I0728965

Sundered

HEARTS

BOOKS BY ANNA J. MCINTYRE

Coulson's Wife

Coulson's Crucible

Coulson's Lessons

Coulson's Secret

Coulson's Reckoning

UNLOCKED HEARTS

Sundered Hearts

After Sundown

While Snowbound

Sugar Rush

UNLOCKED HEARTS

Sundered HEARTS

Anna J. McIntyre

Sundered Hearts
By Anna J. McIntyre
(Unlocked Hearts Series)
A Novel
By Anna J. McIntyre
Cover Design: Elizabeth Mackey
Editor: Suzie O'Connell

Copyright © 2014 Bobbi Holmes
Robeth Publishing, LLC
All Rights Reserved.
www.robeth.com

This novel is a work of fiction.
Any resemblance to places or actual persons,
living or dead is entirely coincidental.
www.robeth.com

ISBN: 978-1-949977-44-8

To Lynn,
Just like Brandon was there for Kit,
you've always been there for me.

I'll think this is funny in a few weeks, Susan Thomas told herself as she left the shelter of her stalled vehicle and began plodding down the muddy dirt road in the midst of a rainstorm. She would discover—in less than an hour—how wrong she was. By the time the year ended, Susan would look back on this day as one of the worst in her entire twenty-six years.

When she got up that morning, there was nothing to indicate this day would be any different from previous days that week. She'd had coffee with her husband Sam and managed to eat a bowl of cereal and a slice of toast before racing off to work at the Ben Franklin Elementary School's attendance office. There hadn't even been any rainclouds in the sky when she'd left that morning.

Her first two hours at work had been fairly typical. Since she worked indoors, she hadn't realized threatening storm clouds had turned the sky gray. It wasn't until Johnny Peters had come walking in the office doorway shortly before lunch that things started to go wrong. He had looked a little green, but she had no idea the second grader was about to projectile vomit in her direction and soak her brand-new silk blouse.

There would be no saving the garment, and since the board of education frowned upon their employees working in just a bra and skirt, she had decided it best if she go home and change clothes. Unfortunately, she hadn't brought a jacket to work that day since it had been clear and sunny when she'd left home that morning. This left her no option but to rinse the silk blouse in the bathroom sink and wear the wet and stinky garment home.

It had started to rain the minute she pulled out of the school parking lot. Initially, the downpour hadn't concerned her; after all, she was snug and dry in her warm car. But then she'd taken a detour due to an accident up ahead on her regular route. There was no other traffic along that stretch of road—just the emergency responders attending to the accident.

For a moment, she had considered waiting—since the detour would take her over a dirt road—but the stench of her blouse made her want to heave, and she'd seen all the vomit that day that she could handle. Against the urgings of that, still silent voice suggesting she wait it out, Susan had turned down the dirt road.

She had soon discovered the rain was quickly turning the dirt road to mud. But it was the dog appearing out of nowhere, who had caused Susan to jerk the steering wheel to one side, landing her in a ditch. There was no way of getting out of the ditch without a tow truck, so she had turned off her engine and grabbed her purse.

Her husband Sam would be at his office. There was no way he was showing property in this weather. She'd give him a call, and he could come pick her up. The moment she had opened her purse, she remembered. She had plugged her cellphone into the charger when she arrived at work that morning, and it was still sitting on the shelf behind her desk— plugged into the wall. Hoping she was wrong, Susan had dumped the contents of her purse onto the passenger seat. No cellphone. Cursing, she then shoved the items back into her purse and did the only thing she could do: walk home in the midst of a rainstorm—without a jacket or umbrella.

Walking along the muddy road wearing heels proved challenging. Wobbling with each step, her long dark hair now drenched, she wished someone would drive by and give her a lift—yet part of her was relieved there was no car in sight.

By the time she reached her street, all she could think of was stripping off her clothes as she walked into her house before racing upstairs to jump in the shower. At this point, she didn't even care if one of the neighbors witnessed her striptease.

She hadn't expected to see Sam's car in the driveway. But it didn't particularly surprise her. He was a real estate agent, and days like this he could work from home using his laptop. In that moment, Susan decided the day's story would have a happy ending. Together, she and Sam could ditch work, pop popcorn, and watch old movies in the den while snuggling by the fireplace.

Giggling, she raced to the side kitchen door. She didn't want to muddy up the front entry. Deciding to surprise her husband, Susan tried to be quiet while unlocking the kitchen door. Tiptoeing into the house, she closed the door behind her. Ducking into the laundry room off the kitchen, she slipped off the wet clothes. Unfortunately, there weren't any dry towels in the laundry room.

Shivering and nude, she raced from the kitchen and peeked into the living room and den. No Sam. Guessing he was upstairs, she moved quietly up the stairway, using all her willpower to suppress her giggles.

When she got to the second floor, she heard Sam's voice. *He must be on the phone,* she thought. But then she heard it—a second voice.

"Sam, I love it when you do that!"

"Do you, baby?"

Feminine giggles.

"Oh, stop, Sam, you're too much!" More giggles.

"I'll show you too much, baby. Now bend over and let Sam the Man take you for a rough ride."

Dazed, unable to comprehend what she was hearing, Susan walked toward the voices. Seconds later—completely nude, her hair drenched—she stood at the doorway to her bedroom. There before her, not six feet away, was her husband preparing to mount from behind a willing and enthusiastic nude woman whom Susan had never seen before.

While Susan did not recognize her husband's lover, she immediately noticed the stark differences between the interloper's body and her own. Although it was impossible to guess the other woman's height, considering the stranger was on her hands and knees, she was obviously much taller than Susan, who stood just five-feet-four-inches tall. Petite Susan, whose trim and fit body—which boasted small but perky breasts that barely filled a B-cup—looked almost childlike compared to this rubenesque woman, whose enormous, full breasts swayed provocatively below the ample body.

The sexual romp came to an abrupt halt when the nude couple on the bed realized they were no longer alone. If the scene had been a movie, the audience would assume something had gone awry in the projection room, because Susan, Sam, and the mystery woman held their places for what seemed like eternity. The only noticeable movement was Sam's erection, which vanished.

As if on cue, they all moved. Sam jumped from the bed, grabbed his jeans off the floor, and pulled them on, not stopping first to put on his briefs. The woman on the bed clutched the sheet to cover herself while glancing frantically around the room, trying to figure out where she'd dropped her clothes.

Of the three, Susan was the only one not trying to hide her nudity. Instead, she reached for the first thing she could find—a music box—and hurled it at Sam's head. He ducked and avoided the missile yet wasn't fast enough to dodge the book she threw his way.

Scrambling from the bed, the mystery woman snatched her clothes off the floor and dashed from the room, grateful Susan was focusing her rage at Sam and not at her. Neither Sam nor Susan seemed to notice that their guest was making a hasty departure.

Sam weaved and bobbed around the bedroom, trying to avoid his wife's rage as she hurled one object after another in his direction. Some made contact; others fell short of their target.

"Damn it, Susan, stop! Are you planning to break everything we own?"

"There is no *we!*" She threw one more object, a small figurine that he had given her on their first Valentine's Day. It flew past his head, hit the wall, and shattered into tiny pieces.

Susan dropped to the floor, wrapped her arms around her nude body and broke into sobs. Closing her eyes tightly, her head bent to the floor, she just wanted to disappear. She wanted to be anywhere but in the bedroom she shared with her cheating husband, the man to whom she had entrusted her heart.

"Ahh, Susan, I'm sorry, baby," Sam muttered.

"Don't call me baby," she managed to say between sobs. *He called* her *baby—the whore he'd just been screwing*, she thought.

"It just hasn't been working for us."

His words were not what she expected to hear. She had expected him to say, *I can explain* or *it's not what you think.*

Sniffling, she wiped her face with the back of her hand and looked up at Sam.

"What do you mean?" she asked.

"It's over, Susan. I want a divorce."

Stunned, Susan stared in disbelief at her husband of almost five years. *A divorce?*

"I'm sorry you found out this way. But maybe it's for the best."

For the best?

"I don't understand?" Susan asked, still dazed.

"I'm in love with Loretta."

"Loretta… the naked woman who just ran out of our bedroom?"

"You can't blame her for running like that. You were acting like a lunatic."

"I was acting like a lunatic?" she squealed in a high pitch voice.

"Pretty much. Look what you did to this room."

Susan glanced around the bedroom. It looked like a battleground. Their personal items littered the floor. Many were broken.

"What are you doing home, by the way? And where are your clothes?"

Susan stared at her cheating husband. She could not believe what he had just asked her. One minute he announces he wants a divorce and in the next asks her why she is home, in a tone that implies she had done something wrong.

Glaring at Sam, Susan got to her feet and marched into the master bathroom off their bedroom, slamming the door behind her, before locking it. She turned on the shower, and when the water was sufficiently warm, she climbed in. The water drenched her, as had the rain less than an hour earlier.

When Susan got out of the shower fifteen minutes later, she toweled off before grabbing her terrycloth robe from the hook on the back of the bathroom door. After slipping on the robe and wrapping a dry towel around her freshly shampooed hair, she stepped out of the bathroom.

Sam sat on the edge of the bed. While she had been in the shower, he had picked the items off the floor, but instead of putting them back where they belonged, he had tossed the unbroken ones on the bed and the broken pieces in the trashcan beside the small desk in their bedroom.

"How long, Sam?"

"Since July."

"You've been seeing her since July? *That's ten months!*" Susan couldn't believe it. In July, they'd celebrated their fourth anniversary and had gone away for a romantic weekend. They'd even discussed the possibility of starting a family.

"I'm sorry, Susan. I never intended to fall in love with her. I just thought it would be a harmless fling."

"*Harmless fling?*" She wanted to start throwing things again. Instead, she asked, "Who is she?"

"Does it matter?"

"I think I have the right to know."

"I met her through work."

"She's another real estate agent?"

"No, she's a title officer. But I don't see where any of that matters." They were silent for a moment. Then he said, "I think you should move out."

"What? You expect me to move out?"

"It is my house," Sam told her.

"*Your house?* I thought it was *our* house."

"I bought this house before we were married."

"You bought this house when we were engaged. We picked it out together." *We fixed it up together.*

"Yes, we were engaged at the time. But I paid for

it with the money I inherited from my grandparents. I'm not trying to be an asshole, Susan, but under community property, the house clearly belongs to me. Not only did I buy it before we were married, I paid for it with money I inherited. But we don't have to talk about this right now. We can discuss this later when you're more rational. I'll stay in the guest room until you find someplace to stay." Sam turned and left the room, leaving Susan standing alone in the bedroom.

CHAPTER TWO

"To your divorce!" Linda raised her wine glass in salute to Susan. The four young women—Linda, Susan, Joyce, and Debbie—sat together at the small round table at the edge of the bar. It was Friday night happy hour at the popular dinner house. The four had been friends since high school.

Less than enthusiastic, Susan half-heartedly raised her glass and gave a little shrug.

"So it's final, then?" Debbie asked. Until Susan's divorce, Debbie had been the only unmarried member of the group.

"It was official on Monday," Susan answered. She set her half-filled wineglass back on the table. It had been almost six months since that fateful day when she had walked in on her cheating husband. *Cheating ex-husband,* she silently reminded herself.

"When does the house close escrow?" Debbie asked.

"Next week," Susan told her. "Sam was pretty pissed the court sided with me and used another real estate agent to list it. He still wasn't over the fact it belonged to both of us, despite his original contention." Susan chuckled and took a sip of wine.

"I never figured out why he thought it was his in the first place," Joyce commented.

"Because," Linda explained, "he bought it before they were married with funds from money he inherited. Even if they were married and he inherited money and used it to buy a house, it would be his and not Susan's."

"Then I don't get it." Joyce frowned. "I thought Susan gets half the money from the sale."

"Ahh, but here's the catch," Linda explained with a chuckle. "There was that pesky commingling of funds!" Linda laughed. Joyce looked confused.

"Joyce, remember, after Sam and I were married, he lost his job and went to real estate school. I was the only one working and paying all the expenses on the house —property tax, insurance, upkeep. Under the law, the house became community property because we spent money I earned on it, which is commingling of funds. Not to mention the fact, I helped refurbish the house."

"Oh." Joyce smiled brightly. "So what're you going to do with your share of the money?"

"Put it in savings for now. If Sam hadn't been such a jerk about everything and the marriage had ended under different circumstances, I'd feel a little funny taking half of the money. It *was* paid for with his inheritance from his grandparents."

"Well, Sam *was* a jerk," Linda told her. "Plus, I remember what that house looked like when you guys bought it."

Susan failed to mention that her half wasn't nearly as much as her friends might imagine. Before dividing proceeds from the sale of their house, debts needed to be paid. Since finding Sam in bed with a strange woman, she'd discovered he'd also run up enormous debts on all their joint credit cards. It was too embarrassing to admit she'd allowed her husband to handle all the household expenses and had never once considered reviewing the accounts. Foolishly, she had trusted Sam with both her heart and her finances.

But, there was enough money for a down payment on a new house, should she ever decide to buy another one again. For now, she would leave the money in her savings account.

Absently, Susan fidgeted with the stem of her wine glass. Looking down at the table, she thought, *I loved that house.* Together, she and Sam had replaced the flooring, painted walls, refinished cabinets. Linda was right. The house belonged as much to her as it did to Sam, regardless of how the marriage had ended.

She had also loved Sam. She had trusted him. Susan had believed their marriage would last forever.

"We're losing her, ladies!" Linda told her friends when she noticed Susan's pensive expression.

"Hey, this is a celebration." Debbie nudged Susan, who forced a smile.

"You're better off without him. Linda is right; Sam was a jerk," Joyce said.

"You guys all liked him when we got married."

"We *tried* to like him for you," Linda insisted.

Susan looked up at Linda and then glanced at her other friends. They wore sheepish expressions.

"Are you saying you *never* really liked him?" Susan asked in disbelief.

Joyce and Debbie gave little shrugs. Susan continued to look from friend to friend.

"Sam was a player. I knew it the minute I met him," Linda explained.

"Why didn't you say anything?"

"We sorta did in the beginning, but you got so mad at us," Joyce reminded her.

Susan considered her words, thinking back to when she had first met Sam during her senior year in college. "It's just that you were always critical of the guys I dated."

"Did you ever consider it might be the guys you

dated and not us just being bitchy?" Debbie asked. Susan didn't respond.

"Okay, first there was Bobby Rogers during our sophomore year in high school," Debbie continued.

"Oh, Bobby Rogers; he was an ass. Wasn't he convicted of inside trading last year?" Joyce asked.

"Hell, we were like fourteen back then," Susan said defensively.

"Let's not forget Adam Klein in your junior year," Debbie went on.

"Adam was nice back then," Susan insisted.

"Susan, Adam was selling coke during our senior year," Linda reminded her.

"He wasn't doing that when I dated him."

"Not that you knew of!" her friends chorused.

"Oh, and how about Jeff Morgan?" Joyce asked.

"Enough!" Susan laughed. "Okay, I get the point. I have shitty taste in men."

"Susan, it's just that you're a nice person and always try to see the best in people," Linda said gently.

"She's right," Joyce agreed.

"You just need to break the pattern. Stop making the same damn mistakes," Debbie told her.

"So, how am I supposed to do that, considering my track record?"

"Stop being so trusting. I mean, it's okay to trust people, but when you first meet a guy, if he's cute and nice to you, all you see is the good," Linda said.

"Yeah, you're kind of a pushover," Debbie agreed.

"Thanks, guys," Susan said sardonically, downing the rest of her wine.

Eventually the conversation drifted from Susan and her poor choice in men. Another round of drinks was served.

"I hate to break this up," Linda said later, glancing at her watch. "But I need to head home. Steve said he'd pick up a pizza tonight for the kids, but I'd like to get home before they go to bed so I can tuck them in."

Linda and Joyce both stood up, each picking up her purse.

"Me, too," Joyce said. "I have no idea what Kevin fed the kids. But he's a big boy; I don't imagine they starved. This was fun, ladies."

Debbie, who remained seated, glanced at Susan, who didn't seem in a hurry to go.

"You don't need to go yet, do you? We could get dinner," Debbie suggested.

"Sounds great," Susan glanced up at her two departing friends. "We'll let you old married women get home to your families while us single ladies tear up the town."

"You do that!" Linda laughed. After exchanging final words and goodbyes, Linda and Joyce left the bar, leaving their two single friends behind.

"Should we eat here?" Susan asked after their friends were gone.

"We might as well. They have good burgers."

"Do you do this often?" Susan asked after picking up a menu from the center of the table.

"Do what?" Debbie grabbed a menu for herself.

"Do the single bar scene."

"Is that what we're doing?" Debbie laughed.

"I don't know." Susan shrugged as she glanced over the menu. "We're both single, and we're in a bar."

"If you mean do I come to bars to meet guys—no. I might meet up with a guy I already know, in a place like this. But do I hook up with guys I meet in a bar? Can't say I ever have. Of course, I have a number of single girlfriends who regularly pick up guys at bars."

"That seems just so… dangerous." Susan cringed. "You know, I wasn't even twenty-one when I met Sam, so I've never gone to a bar as a single woman."

Before Debbie could reply, the waitress walked up to the table to take their orders. When the two friends were alone again, they resumed their conversation.

"Are you nervous, Susan? Being single again?"

"It's just…weird. I never imagined I'd be back dating again."

"Have you gone out with anyone yet?"

"The divorce was just finalized."

"Is that a no? Lots of people date when separated and going through a divorce."

"It just didn't seem right. I think a part of me

hoped I might save my marriage."

"Even after you caught Sam with that woman?"

Susan shrugged and then said, "I know it's crazy. But I didn't want to be a divorced woman. When I married Sam, I naively believed it would be forever. But, I wasn't completely spineless; I never asked Sam to see a marriage counselor or to work on our marriage."

"I don't think that would have been spineless. Lots of people see marriage counselors after an affair, and they make it work."

"True. But the moment Sam told me he no longer loved me, I knew that if we were to somehow save our marriage, he'd have to be the one to come to me and say he'd made a mistake, that he really did still love me."

"I think I can understand that."

"I absolutely refuse to beg for any man's love," Susan said stubbornly. "But that doesn't mean a part of me didn't hope he'd come to some epiphany and realize he did love me and wanted our marriage."

"I'm sorry, Susan."

"Don't feel sorry for me. I'm sorta past all that."

"Are you sure?"

"Yes. The moment I realized Sam was not the man I believed he was—when that finally clicked in—walking away from the marriage was much easier. Of course, I still wish things had been different."

"Now you're single, and it's time to get back out

there!" Debbie cheerfully announced.

"I'm not even sure how to go about doing that."

"I know a few guys—"

"No!" Susan interrupted with a laugh. "I'm not quite ready for any blind dates. I need to get comfortable being alone first before I even consider getting into another relationship."

"Being alone is not all that it's cracked up to be."

"What happen to that guy you were seeing? Stan —right?"

"Oh… Stan. Unfortunately, he turned out to be a little dark."

"Dark? What do you mean?" Susan took a sip of her water.

"I was willing to do a little experimenting—you know—some light bondage, some playful spankings…"

"Oh, Deb, you naughty girl!" Susan laughed.

"Yeah, well, once the play began, Stan wanted to move in a direction I wasn't comfortable with. He wanted me to pick a safe word."

"Safe word? What do you mean?" Susan frowned.

"A safe word, something to say to make him stop if I found the whippings from the riding crop too unbearable."

"He whipped you with a riding crop?"

"No, but he wanted to. I don't mind some fun and games, but real pain—no thank you."

"Was he okay with you breaking it off? He

sounds… kind of scary."

"Oh, he was alright. Stan wasn't an insane person. He wanted to play rough, but he also wanted a consenting partner. We left on good terms, but I'll confess, I was a little nervous when I first broke it off."

"So, that is the kind of thing I have to look forward to?" Susan cringed.

"You just have to be careful and remember not to be so trusting. But that doesn't mean you can't get out there, find the guy who's right for you." Debbie looked over at the door and smiled.

Susan glanced in the direction of Debbie's gaze. Two men had just walked into the bar and headed toward her table. Susan immediately recognized one of the men; it was Debbie's older brother, John. Although she hadn't seen him in a couple years, he looked pretty much as she remembered. Like his sister, he had reddish-brown hair and hazel eyes. Not quite as tall—or as good looking—as his blond companion, he stood several inches less than six feet tall. He was a nice-looking guy, yet not someone she would describe as sexy. *His friend was another matter.*

Susan remembered John had recently gone through a divorce. She also recalled the times he'd pursued her in college, around the same time she had met Sam. She hoped her friend wasn't trying to play Cupid; John wasn't her type. *What is my type*? Susan asked herself.

CHAPTER THREE

"Hey, Susan. Great to see you!" John said when he reached their table. Both he and his friend were dressed similarly, wearing faded denims, tennis shoes, and lightweight jackets over clean cotton button-down shirts. John's hair was damp, and Susan suspected he'd recently stepped out of the shower.

The bar wasn't as busy as it had been when Linda and Joyce had left. Many of the patrons had either moved to the dining room or left the restaurant after having a couple of drinks.

Standing up, she gave him a brief hug and caught the faint scent of cigarette smoke.

"John, wow, it's been a long time," Susan said before sitting back down.

"This is Brandon; he works with me," John introduced as Susan took her seat. "Brandon, this is my sister, Debbie, and Susan—she's an old friend from college."

Brandon said hello and flashed a friendly smile, showing off a set of perfectly straight, white teeth. John and Brandon each took a seat at the table.

"Nice to meet you," Susan and Debbie chorused.

Susan then looked at Debbie and said, "Deb, you didn't mention John would be joining us."

"Oh," Debbie stammered and took a sip of her drink before continuing. "I told him we were going to be here, and if he was out and around, he could stop and say hi. It was nothing definite, so I didn't mention it."

"I thought we were going to After Sundown," Brandon said with a laugh.

"After Sundown?" Susan frowned.

"Oh gosh, do guys still go to that place?" Debbie asked.

"If I did, I'm certainly not telling my sister," John said with a chuckle.

"So, what's After Sundown?" Susan asked again.

"It's an infamous pickup bar," Debbie explained.

"Infamous how?" Susan asked.

"Men and women pretty much go there for one thing: a hookup. No strings booty call. It's a regular hang out for some of the single guys on the construction crew," Debbie explained.

"And how do you know so much about it?" John asked.

"Wouldn't you like to know!" Debbie retorted.

"And you wanted to go there tonight?" Susan asked Brandon.

"Not really; I was just joking." He shrugged.

"I guess I sorta figured most bars were pickup bars, if you were to go alone," Susan said.

"Or with a friend." Brandon grinned.

"Then I suppose it's a good thing Debbie's big brother is here to protect us from those who might get the wrong idea," Susan said playfully before glancing around the bar and noticing there didn't seem to be anyone she needed protection from. Most of the remaining bar clientele was paired, and those who weren't were already engrossed in their own private conversations.

"I'm not your brother," John reminded her.

"Where are you working now?" Susan asked, ignoring his comment.

"Still in construction."

"Yeah, that teacher's credential paid off," Debbie teased.

"Shut up," John said with a laugh, obviously not insulted.

"That's right, you were going to be a teacher," Susan recalled.

"I guess you might say I came to realize I hate kids." They all laughed.

The waitress arrived with the burgers for Susan and Debbie. After serving the meals and taking drink and food orders from John and Brandon, she left the table.

"I've been working construction since high school. When teaching didn't pan out, I went back to it. Figured I'd do it until I decided what I wanted to do with my degree but ended up staying. Pays well," John explained.

"You know, Susan works for the local school district," Debbie reminded her brother.

"My condolences," John said.

"Yeah, I guess I'm not the only one who isn't using her degree," Susan said before taking a bite of her burger.

"Remind me, what was your major?" John asked.

"Business major, I'm embarrassed to admit."

"Why embarrassed?" Brandon asked.

"Because I'm working in the attendance office of an elementary school and not using my degree."

"Seems like an honest job," Brandon said with an encouraging smile. Susan couldn't help but notice his lively blue eyes. *He is a cutie*, she thought.

"It pays the bills. I got married right after college and was just starting to send out resumes when my husband lost his job. He decided he wanted to go into real estate. I grabbed the first paying job I could land so he could go to real estate school. I just never left. I suppose time has a way of getting away from us."

"I have to say, you two make me feel a little better

about not going to college," Brandon said with a grin. "Look at all that money I saved."

"Yeah, there is that." Susan took a sip of her drink. "So, you've always been in construction?"

"Not really. You might say I grew up in the restaurant business. My first job was a busboy in my parent's restaurant. But I hated it. I like working with my hands, and frankly, dealing with customers is not something I enjoy. I was thrilled when I landed my first job in construction and had an excuse *not* to work in the family restaurant."

"Did that make your parents sad?" Susan asked.

"I don't think so. They had my older sister—who did go into the family business. But my folks are gone now and so is the restaurant."

"I'm sorry," Susan said.

"I miss my folks. As for the restaurant, I felt bad for my sis—she loved it—but after the folks were gone, with Dad's medical expenses and all, she just couldn't hold onto it. But don't feel too sorry for her. She's happy with her life now."

"I'm glad it worked out for her," Debbie said. "See, Susan, it's not too late. You're starting a new chapter in your life, so why not a new job?"

Brandon looked inquisitively at Susan.

"This past Monday my divorce was finalized," Susan explained.

"There is life after divorce, trust me," John told her.

"How long has it been for you?" Susan asked.

"About a year now. She got married last month."

"I'm sorry. I hadn't heard." Susan hadn't realized it had been that long.

"Hey, I'm just glad we didn't have any kids," John said.

"Do you have children?" Brandon asked Susan.

"No. I suppose John's right; things would be much more difficult if there were kids in the picture."

Before Susan could respond, the server brought John and Brandon their beers.

"What is Sam doing these days?" John asked after the server left.

"John, don't ask her that!" Debbie scolded.

"That's okay, Deb. It's no secret. He's living with Loretta."

"Loretta?"

"It's Sam's skank," Debbie told her brother.

"Deb, I've never called her a skank." Susan didn't want to sound bitter.

"No, you didn't. I gave her that name."

"Now that your divorce is finalized, you think he'll be getting remarried?" John asked.

"I'm not sure." Susan took a sip of her drink. She didn't feel comfortable with the conversation, and her answer was less than truthful. From what she'd heard through mutual friends, Sam and Loretta's relationship was on rocky ground. Apparently, living together fulltime had taken a bite out of the romance and cooled down the once hot affair.

After the court had allowed Susan to stay in the house until it sold, Sam had moved into Loretta's small apartment. Sam hadn't intended to downsize his home, and Loretta had been looking forward to moving into Sam's house. To complicate matters, the real estate market had slowed, which meant Loretta had lost her job at the title company while Sam's commissions had begun shrinking, and he no longer had a wife's salary to fall back on during a downturn in the market. It wasn't a scenario either had bargained for.

"When are you moving out of your house?" Debbie asked Susan.

"Escrow closes next week, and I wanted to move on Sunday. But the guy I hired called me this morning with some lame excuse as to why he can't make it. I'll figure out something tomorrow."

"Where are you moving?" John asked.

"I rented an apartment across town. I'm not taking much furniture. Sam and I divided it up a few months ago and sold what neither of us wanted. I have mostly boxes, so I suppose I can move most of it myself. It'll just take longer, and I'll need to take a few days off work."

"I could help," John offered. "I'm sure I can find someone with a truck."

"I have a truck. I'll help," Brandon offered. "I'm not doing anything on Sunday."

"Oh, Sunday… I forgot…" John began.

"Hey, no problem," Susan told him. "I'll figure out something. It was sweet of you guys to offer."

"No, I can help," John insisted. "It just has to be in the morning. I have a side job in the afternoon, and I can't put it off."

"I can be there in the morning, too," Brandon said.

"See, Brandon has offered his truck," John said with a smile. "No reason to worry about it. We can get you moved Sunday morning."

"Okay, if you guys are sure. I'll be happy to pay you."

"We don't want your money," John insisted.

"But we will move for beer," Brandon added with a laugh.

"I can do beer!" Susan said. "But only if you promise to wait until after the move before you drink it."

"Deal," Brandon promised.

John stood up, reached in his jacket pocket, and pulled out a pack of cigarettes.

"I'm going outside to have a smoke before they bring our burgers," John explained.

"Those things will kill you," Susan teased. John returned with a shrug and made his way outside.

"Sorry to see John's still smoking," Susan told

Debbie after he went outside. She then looked to Brandon and asked, "Do you smoke?"

"Me? No. Never did."

Debbie looked at Susan and said, "Maybe you can get him to quit."

"Why would he quit for me?" Susan frowned.

"He's always liked you."

Brandon sipped his beer and silently listened to the exchange.

"Don't play matchmaker, Deb. I've always liked your brother, but not in that way. And I already told you, it's way too soon for me to even think about dating again." Susan glanced at Brandon and blushed, suddenly embarrassed.

"Please don't repeat what I said," Susan asked Brandon.

"You don't want John to know you aren't interested?" he asked.

"No… I mean… Hell, I doubt John is interested, but that's not the point. Deb here loves to play matchmaker, and I imagine he'd be embarrassed and annoyed if he knew his little sister was trying to hook us up."

"I doubt that," Brandon murmured before downing the rest of his beer.

CHAPTER FOUR

Susan stood at her living room window looking outside, cursing the rain. What did she expect? It was November. Not ideal weather for moving, but escrow would be closing in a couple of days, and she had to be out by then. She wondered if Brandon and John would even show up.

By the time she finished her second cup of coffee, her question was answered. She watched as John's Jeep pulled up in front of her house, followed by Brandon's red pickup truck.

"Sorry about the weather," Susan apologized when she answered the door a few minutes later.

"It is a bitch, but not much you can do about it," John said as he walked into the house.

"I grabbed some tarps," Brandon said as he followed John inside. "I'll try to keep your boxes dry as much as possible.

Susan had already stacked her boxes neatly in the living room. But it was the furniture John and Brandon decided to move first. They ended up making numerous trips back and forth between the house and apartment, taking all three of their vehicles, filling each one completely.

"I NEED TO GET OUT OF HERE," JOHN SAID, GLANCING AT his watch as he stood in Susan's front entry several hours later.

"Oh, that's right. I forgot you have a job this afternoon. I didn't realize it would take this long," Susan apologized.

"I was happy to help, honestly. I just wish I didn't have to take off on you."

"It's only one more load; I can handle it," Brandon offered.

"Thanks, Brandon, I owe you," John said.

"Hey, let me get you that beer I promised."

"That's okay. I'll get it later. I really don't want to show up on the job with beer," John said with a laugh.

Susan walked John to the front door. They stood in the open doorway and looked outside. The sun appeared to have pushed the gray clouds aside. It was no longer raining.

"Have you tried that new Japanese restaurant that opened up by your new apartment?" John asked.

"No. To be honest, I didn't notice it."

"I was thinking, why don't we try it out next Friday night?" John asked.

"Friday…" Susan stammered, her mind scrambling for a graceful way to decline his invitation, especially since he'd just helped her move. Brandon was busy hauling boxes from the house to the truck and had just picked up one of the last boxes from the adjoining room when John extended his invitation. She was fairly certain Brandon overheard. Susan wished she and John could discuss this in private, as she had no desire to embarrass John—or herself.

"Gee, thanks John, that's sweet of you," Susan began. "But I'm afraid I have a million things to do this week, what with moving an all. Plus, next week is Thanksgiving, and I already promised my mother I'd help her. We have a bunch of family coming in for the holiday."

"No problem, I understand. How about I give you a call after Thanksgiving?"

"Sure. Don't forget I need to get you that beer."

John leaned toward Susan and whispered, "I don't care about the beer. There's something else that interests me." Before she could respond, he brushed a kiss across her cheek and then turned and made a hasty exit. Stunned, Susan stood at the doorway and watched John as he got into his car and drove away.

"That was awkward," Brandon said. He stood behind Susan in the entry, holding a box. She turned abruptly and faced him.

"You heard?" she asked.

"Yep, sure did." He set the box back down on the floor. "You aren't interested, are you?"

"No, but I don't want to hurt his feelings. I guess it was wrong of me to let him help me today."

"Why do you say that?"

"Because I sorta knew he was interested in me."

"Hey, he offered to help. It's not like you were flirting with him."

"I sure hope I didn't come across like that," Susan said. "Are you two very good friends?"

"John and me?" Brandon laughed. "To be honest, I barely know him. We just happened to work on the same job last week. On Friday, he was trying to get someone to go to the bar so he could see you."

"What do you mean *see me*?"

"He already knew you were going to be there, but he didn't want to show up alone. I guess his sister called him. He tried to get one of his friends to go, but they were all already doing something. When he asked me, I figured sure, why not? I was curious to see who this girl was he was so anxious to see again."

"Damn…"

"Hey, he'll get over it. And who knows? When you've moved past your divorce, maybe you'll be interested in him. He seems like a nice guy."

"No... I mean he is nice. I've known him forever, and his sister is a good friend. But, no, John really is not my type. Plus, he smokes."

"Yeah, smoking is a deal killer for me, too."

"Are you hungry?" Susan asked.

"Hungry?"

"Yeah. We've been working all morning, and I don't know about you, but all I had for breakfast was cereal. I haven't cleaned out the fridge yet, and I've got lunchmeat in there, and some salad. Would you like a sandwich?"

"Sure, if you're going to have one. I'm kind of hungry, too."

Twenty minutes later, Brandon and Susan sat on the kitchen floor together, each eating a ham sandwich.

"Thanks for all your help today; I appreciate it." Susan took a bite of her sandwich as she leaned against a cabinet.

"No problem. Although, you took a risk letting me help you."

"Umm, how so?" Susan looked nervously at Brandon. According to Brandon's own admission, John barely knew him. As far as she knew, Brandon could be some serial rapist, and here she was, alone with him in her kitchen. What had her friends just told her? *You are too trusting.*

"One summer," Brandon began, not noticing Susan's uneasy expression, "one of my friends picked up this cute girl at a bar. That was a Friday night. They spent the night together—at her place. On Saturday morning, she told him she and her roommate were moving to another place in the next town. Of course, he volunteered to help, and since I had a truck, he volunteered me. The roommate was pretty hot, so I figured, why not? We loaded her dining table in the back of my truck—and she tells us it belonged to her grandma so be careful. Of course, we didn't think it was necessary to tie the thing down."

"Oh no…" Susan's eyes widened.

"You should have seen that thing fly out of my truck on the freeway. Damn lucky it didn't hit someone. Broke into a million pieces; scattered like a giant box of toothpicks."

"What did she say?"

"I imagine it wasn't G-rated. They were behind us when it happened, so they saw it fly off. My friend was with me in the truck, so we turned off the freeway and got the hell out of there. My friend never saw the girl again."

"That is awful!" Susan laughed. "I'm surprised they didn't track you two down!"

"I know. My friend and I never went back to the bar where he met her. Can't say I blame them for being pissed at us. It was a pretty lame. But we were young and dumb."

"After that experience, I'm surprised you even volunteered to help me."

"I not only brought tarps today, I brought rope in case you had a dining room table to move. I learned my lesson."

"I do appreciate your help."

"This is a great house, by the way. Are you sad to let it go?" Brandon glanced around the room.

"In a way. It was a mess when we bought it."

"You refurbished it?"

"Pretty much." Susan glanced down at the faux wood floor and recalled the old linoleum tile they'd painstakingly removed one weekend.

"Who did the work?"

"My ex and I did most of it. This floor we're sitting on—I helped put it down."

"Nice," Brandon glanced down, casually inspecting the workmanship.

"What exactly do you do in construction?"

"I'm a framer. Although, I'd love to be in the position to buy houses to remodel and flip."

"When we were fixing up this house, I thought about that, too. My ex is a Realtor, so I figured it would be a natural fit."

"What did he think?"

"Oh, Sam wasn't interested. Refurbishing this house might have been a labor of love for me, but for Sam… He just wanted to get it done. In the middle of the remodel, he told me he would never again buy a fixer-upper. Claimed it was too much work."

"I suppose it is. But it's the kind of work I enjoy."

"Me, too." Susan glanced around the kitchen and gave a little sigh. "I love this house, but even if I could keep it, I don't think I would."

"Too many memories?"

"Too many fake memories."

Brandon frowned.

"My marriage—my ex—weren't what I thought they were. He wasn't who I thought he was. Someday, I can get another house."

"And another husband?"

"I don't know. I'm not in a rush to jump back into the dating game. I was serious when I told Debbie I wanted to get used to being alone first."

"That's probably a good idea. And if John's serious about you, then I imagine he'd appreciate you giving it some time."

"I don't know what you mean."

"If you're serious about someone, the last thing you'd want is to be the rebound lover."

"Rebound lover?"

"Yeah. The first one someone goes to after a breakup. They never work out—at least not in the long term."

"You'd never want to be a rebound lover?" Susan asked.

"Considering where I am in life, a rebound lover would probably be the best option."

"Ah, you're just looking for fun without commitment."

Brandon smiled sheepishly and gave a little shrug. "Hey, I'm a dog, what can I say?"

"That's right, you did mention you wanted to go to that bar—what was it called—After Sundown?"

"Hey," Brandon said with a laugh. "I said I was just joking."

"Ah, but were you really?" Susan asked with a grin. "Fess up, you've been there before."

Brandon didn't answer immediately, but then he looked up with a grin. "Yeah, I go sometimes—but just to play pool."

"Yeah, sure—*the pool.*" Susan laughed. "Tell me the truth. Does John go there, too?"

"Thought you weren't interested in John."

"I'm not. I'm just nosey."

"I honestly don't know if he goes there or not. But if you're interested in him, I'll be happy to help out my good buddy John."

"John? Help him how? I thought you didn't know him that well?"

"I'll volunteer to be your rebound lover. That way, when you're ready to date John, all that rebound stuff will be out of your system."

"Wow, that is sweet of you," Susan chuckled. "You were serious when you said you were a dog, weren't you?"

"Pretty much." Brandon gave her a wink.

"Thanks for the generous offer, but I'm not really interested in John."

"I'd still be willing to volunteer," Brandon quipped.

Instead of laughing, Susan eyed Brandon curiously. "Umm… I've been out of the… game for a while. Is that… Are you hitting on me?"

"Not so much hitting," Brandon said seriously. "But letting you know I'd be interested if you ever…I find you very attractive. I know you aren't in the place to start a serious relationship, and frankly, neither am I. But, well…. Just letting you know."

Brandon stood up quickly and tossed his napkin into the trashcan. "We should probably get the rest of your stuff moved before it starts raining again."

Susan stood up and gave him a nod, feeling suddenly awkward. Brandon must have sensed her unease because he then said, "Hey, Susan, I didn't mean to make you feel uncomfortable. Forget I said anything. It's all cool. But I just thought I'd let you know I was interested if you ever were."

CHAPTER FIVE

Several days before Thanksgiving, Susan dropped a case of beer off at Debbie's apartment and asked her to give it to John when she saw him on Thursday. She needed to pay her moving debt, yet she didn't want to drop the beer off at John's house and give him the wrong impression.

As promised, John called Susan after Thanksgiving in spite of the fact Susan had made it clear to Debbie that she wasn't interested in dating her brother. John called the next week and then the next. But after the third call, he decided she must be serious, so he didn't call the following week.

What Susan didn't tell her friend—or anyone—was that she was disappointed she hadn't run into Brandon again. She couldn't help but think about what he had said—what he had offered—not that she was actually considering such a relationship. He was clearly offering to be her—what was it they called it —*fuck buddy*. A less crude term was *friends with benefits*, but she didn't think he was offering his friendship.

Not once did he stop by her apartment or make some excuse to see her. One day, when thinking of Brandon, Susan realized she didn't even know his last name. If she wanted to contact him, there was no way to do so—even if she called John. According to Brandon, the two men barely knew each other. What she did find herself doing was checking out red pickup trucks. If she passed one on the road, her blood pressure spiked.

When Christmas break arrived, she stopped thinking of the hunky framer, and her mind drifted to other thoughts. Last year during this time, she and Sam had driven to a Christmas tree farm and picked out their tree together. She'd gotten rid of most of her Christmas ornaments—she'd collected them with Sam and couldn't bear the thought of hanging them on another Christmas tree.

She was alone in her kitchen fixing a pot of tea when the doorbell rang. Turning off the stove, she went to answer the door. Peering out the peephole, she was surprised to see who was standing on her front porch.

"Sam? What are you doing here?" Susan asked the moment she opened the door.

"I just wanted to talk. Can I come in?" Dressed

casually in jeans and a sweater, it didn't look as if he'd come from his office.

"I suppose," Susan said hesitantly, opening the door wider. "How did you know where I lived?"

"Our Realtor."

"Gee, I thought they had to keep those things confidential," she muttered before closing the door behind them and leading Sam into her living room. She sat down, curious as to what he had to say. Not waiting to be asked, Sam sat down on a chair across from Susan.

"I've left Loretta," he blurted out.

"Oh, really?" Susan wondered why he was telling her.

"I screwed up, Susan."

"Yes, you did. So?"

"I want to come back."

"Excuse me?" She sat up straighter in the chair.

"I said I want to come back. I'm sorry I hurt you, but I want us to work it out."

"Sam, if you haven't noticed, our divorce is finalized. Our house is gone. There is no *us*."

"I figure we have the money from the sale of the house. I'll find us another one…"

"Wait a minute. You honestly expect me to take you back? After everything that happened, everything you said?"

"I know I said some stupid stuff, but you ended up getting your way. You got to stay in the house, you pretty much picked the real estate agent. I split my referral with you."

"So because of that, you think I should take you back?"

"It's not like you got screwed in the divorce or anything. I messed up, Susan. I've admitted it; can't we just move past that? People get remarried all the time. If you hadn't been in such a damn hurry to finalize the divorce, we'd be separated now, and we could just move back in together and get on with our lives. I know this complicates things a little, but it's doable."

"Sam, where are you living?"

"Living? I told you, I left Loretta."

"I got that. But where are you living right now? I understood you were living at her apartment."

"Yeah, well, I'm not living there anymore."

"You aren't answering my question. Where are you staying tonight?"

"Tonight? I was hoping here, with you."

Susan stood up abruptly.

"This conversation is over," she announced.

"What do you mean, over?" Sam reluctantly got to his feet.

"Sam, it's over. I don't love you anymore. I have no desire to live with you—to marry you again. I hope you find some happiness, but you won't find it with me."

Without waiting for his reply, she marched to the front door and threw it open.

"Goodbye, Sam."

"You're serious," Sam stammered, clearly not expecting her reaction.

"Very."

<hr>

"HE EXPECTED YOU TO LET HIM MOVE IN WITH YOU?" Linda asked. She and Susan sat at Starbucks, each drinking a cup of coffee.

"Apparently so." Susan absently stirred her drink.

"What an ass. So, he and Loretta are finished?"

"Who knows? I wouldn't be surprised if he went back there since he needs a place to stay."

"Were you tempted?"

"Tempted?"

"I remember there was a time you hoped he'd come to his senses and come back to you—tell you he had made a mistake. Isn't that what he did today?"

"Are you saying I should have taken him back?"

"Of course not. I just wanted to know how *you* felt about all of it."

"I…" Susan stared down into her coffee as she considered the question. Finally, she looked up and said, "I felt nothing. Absolutely nothing."

"Nothing?"

"Surprised the hell out of me, Linda. But nothing. Part of me was asking myself—*did you really love this jerk?* It was like I was seeing Sam for the very first time, and I didn't like what I saw."

"Good girl!" Linda cheered, lifting her coffee cup in a mock salute.

"What are you so happy about?" Susan chuckled and took a sip of her coffee.

"You're over him. Really over him."

Susan smiled and looked up at her friend. "You know, I think you're right. So, what now?"

"Now you get on with your life."

"I thought I was doing that."

"You know what I mean. Think about dating again."

"I will if you promise not to tell John I'm ready to start dating."

Linda laughed, and then asked, "Has he called you again?"

"No, not since the last time I told you about. But I don't want to hurt his feelings—or Deb's. But seriously, it was like college all over again."

"Yeah, Johnny Boy did have the hots for you back then."

"I'll tell you a secret," Susan whispered.

"What?"

"I know this sounds awful… but you know what I really miss?"

"Sex?"

"How did you know I was going to say that?"

"Well, how long has it been since you've been with anyone?"

"Anyone? You mean with Sam. Let's see… I don't know… almost eight months, I guess."

"Eight months! Lordy, girl, you need to get laid!"

"I know… I do!" Susan broke into giggles. "Is that awful for me to say?"

"Nahh, according to *Cosmopolitan,* you're in your sexual prime. Or was that *Good Housekeeping*? So, tell me, did seeing Sam again get you horny? This is the first time you've talked like this… at least to me."

"Sam? God no! But I suppose… well… seeing him again and not feeling anything, not wanting him…it sorta liberated me. Made me realize I've every right to feel those things again. Even if it's just lust."

"Whatever you do, make sure he wears a condom. I know you're on the pill. But still, play it safe."

"Yes, *Mom.*"

"Anyone you interested in?"

"You mean for a booty call?" Susan chuckled.

"Yes."

"No… well… that's not entirely true. There was this one guy."

"Go on…"

"He's the one John brought to the bar that night."

"Oh, the surfer dude. Debbie said he was hot."

"She called him a surfer dude?"

"I think I heard you call him that, too."

"I might have. He did remind me of the quin-tessential sexy beach bum. Blond hair that needed trimming, hunky tanned bod, and sexy blue eyes."

"Said she would have been all over that, but the guy spent the entire night checking you out."

"She said that?"

"Yep."

"I didn't notice him checking me out—or giving me any more attention than Debbie." *At least not at the bar*, Susan told herself.

"Didn't he offer to help you move?"

"Yes, but... It doesn't matter. I don't even know his last name."

"Isn't he a friend of John's?"

"Not really. They had just met through work. But even if he was, I can't exactly ask John. I don't even know Brandon's last name. I just know he works in construction as a framer."

"But he was hot?"

"Very. But honestly, Linda, I'm just being silly. It's not like I'm going to hunt down some man I barely know and drag him off to bed."

"Maybe not. But at least now, if the opportunity comes up, go for it!"

"Yeah, right." Susan laughed. "Thanks for meeting me here. It's nice having someone to talk to."

"I'm always here for you. So, what are you going to do now?"

"Now? I think I'm going to go buy a Christmas tree, pick up some new ornaments, go back to my apartment, and maybe bake some chocolate chip cookies."

CHAPTER SIX

Susan celebrated Christmas with her family. On Christmas Eve, she went to church with her parents, something she and Sam used to do together. He didn't show up at the church service, and according to the grapevine, he had returned to Loretta. She couldn't help but feel sorry for both Sam and Loretta. Susan realized she would prefer to be alone rather than be with someone she didn't love and respect. She felt neither love nor respect for Sam.

Linda and her husband hosted a New Year's Eve party at their house, which Susan attended. She spent most of the evening dodging unwanted advances from John, who had had too much to drink. But she did accept a date from another man at the party.

Susan's date was uneventful, and by the end of the evening, she knew she wouldn't accept a second date should he ask—which he did. By the time Valentine's Day rolled around, she'd gone out on three different dates—with three different men—and none did she wish to repeat. The furthest any of the dates went was a goodnight kiss.

In spite of her dismal dating record, Susan was willing to keep trying. She figured there had to be some guy out there who was worth a second date. So far, she hadn't found one she wanted to sleep with, yet that didn't mean she didn't want to have sex. Susan definitely wanted to have sex—just not with any of the men she'd gone out with.

On the first Friday in March, Susan met Debbie for drinks after work. She'd just finished a glass of wine when John *happened* to drop by. Susan fabricated an excuse to leave prematurely, saying she was going to her sister's for dinner, and made her exit.

It is a shame John doesn't appeal to me sexually, Susan told herself. She thought it might be nice to have a friend to call up for a booty call when needed. *Like I would actually do that,* she laughed to herself.

Driving down the street she noticed a bar—After Sundown. *Why does that sound familiar?* she asked herself. Just as she was about to pass its parking lot's entrance, she noticed a red pickup truck—Brandon's red truck. Without thinking, Susan turned into the parking lot.

She just sat there a minute, her heart pounding. Did she dare go into the bar? Going into a bar alone wasn't something she would normally do, but

Brandon was inside, so she should be safe—at least she hoped so.

Mustering her courage, Susan thought, *What the hell* and got out of her parked car. She walked to the bar's entrance. The moment she walked into the smoky room, it came back to her—*After Sundown*, the infamous pickup bar.

It took a moment for her eyes to adjust to the dim lighting. Country music blared from the jukebox while several couples danced toward the back of the room, their movements more reminiscent of sexual intercourse than conventional dance steps. Some of the clientele played pool while others sat at the bar or at picnic tables. Eyes turned in her direction as she walked toward the bar. She could feel them checking her out.

Nervously, she approached the bartender. The bar top separated them. Her eyes searched the dark room for Brandon, but she didn't see him. Susan began to wonder if she'd made a mistake coming into After Sundown alone.

"What can I get you?" the bartender asked.

"Vodka tonic, please," she said nervously.

"I'll get it for her," a gravelly male voice called out. Susan looked toward the voice. The man reminded her of someone who'd just been released from prison. His baldhead glistened with sweat while one side of his neck sported an unattractive demonic tattoo. It appeared his nose had suffered one too many breaks and she wondered if the bulging biceps were the product of a prison gym. *What the hell am I doing here?*

She was about to decline the drink offer when she heard another voice call out.

"No, she's with me. I got it." It was Brandon's voice. "Hi, sugar. I wondered what was taking you so long," Brandon said, speaking loudly for the benefit of Susan's unsavory suitor.

The bald man grumbled, yet didn't argue. She turned toward Brandon.

"Brandon…"

"What the hell are you doing here?" Brandon hissed.

"I… I saw your truck. Just thought I would stop in and say hi." She felt foolish.

Brandon took the empty bar stool next to Susan and leaned close to her.

"Did you forget what we said about this place?" he asked.

"I sort of forgot," she said guiltily. The bartender set a cocktail on the bar top in front of her. She grabbed it and took a sip.

"What are *you* doing here?" she asked, looking down at her drink.

"I'm horny," Brandon snapped.

Startled by his answer, she quickly turned in his direction and eyed him curiously. He looked more angry than horny.

"Maybe that's why I'm here."

"Well, sweetheart, by the way all the men are checking you out, you shouldn't have a problem getting what you came here for."

"That sounds disgusting," she said, now feeling embarrassed.

"You said it," he reminded.

"You started it."

"Did I? I don't recall dragging you in here," he said.

She could smell whisky on his breath and wondered if he was drunk. He hadn't been surly when they'd first met. He'd been funny, sweet, and sexy. He was still sexy. In fact, he was sexier than she remembered. The temptation to run her hands through his messy blond hair was almost too much to resist—but she did.

While she didn't find inebriated men attractive, something about Brandon made her restless—needy. *Good lord, I am a slut!* Susan took another sip of her drink. In her head, she calculated how long it had been since she'd had sex. Almost a year of celibacy for a woman nearing her twenty-seventh birthday was definitely too long.

"You want to come home with me?" Susan blurted out. Her question startled Brandon as much as it did her. However, Brandon didn't spend his time considering what she'd just asked. Instead, he stood up, dug one hand in his pocket, and pulled out some money. After slamming the bills on the bar to pay for the drinks, he grabbed Susan's hand and pulled her off the barstool, leading her toward the exit.

She insisted on taking her car, believing he had had too much to drink. Sitting sideways in the passenger seat, Brandon watched Susan as she drove the vehicle.

"Do you always pull men out of bars?" he asked, sounding more amused than concerned.

"Actually, you're the first one," she said nervously, trying to keep her eyes on the road. The way he stared at her sent chills up the back of her neck.

"I can't wait until I can take your clothes off," he told her, his voice low. Brandon reached out and fingered the button on her blouse, then dropped his hand down to her skirt, touching its hem and running his fingertips up her thigh under the skirt's fabric.

"Umm… I think we should wait until we get to my apartment," Susan stammered.

"I'm not good at waiting," Brandon whispered, leaning toward her, kissing the side of her neck. The sensation sent goose bumps over her sensitive skin.

"Stop that; you're going to make me get into an accident," she whispered.

Brandon chuckled, then moved his hand back to her blouse and unbuttoned the front.

"I'm serious, Brandon. It's hard for me to concentrate," she warned.

"You make me hard, so it's only fair." He laughed and slipped his hand inside her blouse. She wanted to close her eyes and savor the sensation as his fingers wiggled their way inside her bra cup, before nudging her breast from its lacy restraint. His hand covered her right breast and gave it a gentle squeeze. The sensation made her gasp.

"You have amazing breasts."

She almost said they were too small, but by the way his hand moved over her breast, it was obvious he liked what he found. By the time they reached her apartment, he'd unsnapped the front of her bra, freeing both breasts and doing his best to make her nipples hard and erect.

When she parked the car and turned off the ignition, he moved closer and kissed her lips roughly, pressing his eager tongue inside her mouth before abandoning her lips and moving downward for her nipples. He'd already opened her blouse, exposing her breasts when his mouth claimed her left nipple, and then the right, gently sucking and licking the taut pink nubs.

Closing her eyes, Susan leaned back in her car seat, ignoring the possibility that someone might walk past her carport. But, it was dark outside, so she pushed such thoughts from her mind.

Abruptly, Brandon sat back up and pulled her blouse closed.

"Let's get inside," he told her. It sounded more like an order than a request, but she complied.

Susan didn't bother to take the time to re-button her blouse for the short walk to her front door. Once they were inside, Brandon's hand reached for her blouse and stripped it off. He did the same to her bra, dropping both garments on the entry floor.

Tossing her purse to a nearby table, Susan reached for Brandon's shirt collar as she kicked off her shoes. He kissed her mouth again as eager hands assisted in the undressing. They slowly made their way toward her bedroom.

By the time they were at Susan's bedside, all but Susan's panties were removed. Brandon lost his shirt and shoes in the entry, and his denims were unzipped. He tugged down his jeans as his eyes fixed on Susan, who stood before him wearing only her silk panties. Her nipples glistened from his wet kisses.

"You are so hot," Brandon said breathlessly as he hastily tugged off his jeans and sat on the side of her bed, wearing just his white briefs.

Standing before Brandon's spread knees, Susan looked down and noticed his erect penis had escaped the fly of the briefs and was standing impressively at attention. Brandon reached for her hips and pulled her toward him, tugging down her panties.

"Damn, they are so wet." Brandon laughed.

Susan blushed and pushed Brandon back onto the bed, climbing atop him. Impatient, she tugged off his briefs and forgot about Linda's warning about condoms. Positioning herself atop Brandon, Susan took the dominate position and pressed herself onto his erection. Closing his eyes, Brandon reached out and grabbed hold of Susan's hips, gently guiding her onto him.

Once they were joined, it became a frantic, demanding ride. When Brandon felt Susan's release squeezing him, he couldn't restrain himself a moment longer and found his own bit of heaven.

Exhausted, Susan lay sprawled atop Brandon, still joined, not wanting to pull away. Breathing heavily, Brandon closed his eyes and stroked Susan's bare back.

"Are you on birth control?" he asked at last.

"Yes," she said, not opening her eyes.

Brandon's hands moved to her bare bottom, pulling her closer, reminding them both that they were still joined.

Sometime later, they took a shower together and then made love for a second time. At midnight, they slipped out to the kitchen and ate sandwiches before going back to bed and having sex for a third time.

When Susan woke the next morning, Brandon was gone, but there was a note by the bed.

I thought I better go pick up my truck before it gets

towed. I called a cab. Thanks for last night. I will call you – Brandon.

Sitting up in the bed, reading the note, Susan realized she still didn't know Brandon's last name. She also didn't have his phone number—nor did he have hers.

"Well, he knows where I live," Susan said aloud. Smiling, she laid back on the mattress, feeling deliciously alive and satisfied—and just a little bit sore. She knew it was stupid to have unprotected sex, especially with a guy she barely knew and had found hanging out at a notorious pickup bar, but she pushed that thought from her mind, choosing instead to savor the sensual memories from the previous night.

It was never like that with Sam, she thought.

CHAPTER SEVEN

"Did you hear John got a new job and is moving to Texas?" Linda told Susan the following week when they met for lunch.

"Texas? No, I hadn't heard, but I haven't talked to Debbie this week. What kind of a job? Is it in construction?"

"No. It's some sort of sales job in the educational field. He starts next week. I guess he won't be pestering you anymore."

"Wow, that was sudden. I hope it works out for him. I'm going to look for a new job when school's out this summer."

"You won't miss summers off?" Linda asked while glancing over the menu.

"I suppose so, but I need to make more money, and I only took the job because Sam wanted to go to real estate school."

"Hey, speaking of real estate, did Sam know that Realtor who was killed the other day?"

"I don't know. I haven't talked to him. But I didn't recognize his name."

"Kevin Landon, the paper said. It's so sad. He was married, had a little girl. Scum killed him for what, twenty bucks?"

"At least they caught the guy."

"I hope they fry him… You look really good, by the way."

"Thanks, I feel great." Susan grinned.

"You seeing anyone?"

"Sort of."

"Anyone I know?"

"Not exactly."

"Sort of… Not exactly… Come on girl, what's going on?" Linda urged.

"I sort of hooked up with Brandon."

"Brandon the hot surfer dude?"

"I don't even know if he surfs." Susan laughed. "But yeah, Friday night. He… umm… he spent the night with me."

"Wow. So, when are you seeing him again?"

"He said he would call me."

"You know, you can call him."

"That would be easier if I actually had his number." *Or knew his last name.*

"You really like this guy?"

"To be honest, I don't really know him that well. But yeah, I like what I know so far."

"Hey, remember what we told you."

"What?" Susan wondered if Linda was going to remind her to wear a condom again—and she certainly wasn't about to admit she had been foolish enough to have sex three times, without a condom.

"Don't be too trusting."

"Oh, that. Yeah, I know."

"What do you know about him?"

"He's a framer... never went to college. His parents are dead. He has a sister. He's a great kisser..."

"Is he married?"

"Married? Why would you ask that? I wouldn't go out with a married guy."

"Did you ask him?"

"Ask him? No. But he wasn't wearing a wedding ring."

"So? Construction workers rarely wear wedding rings; it's too dangerous," Linda insisted.

"I didn't ask him if he was married. I just assumed he wasn't."

"Why, because he hit on you?"

"If I'm honest, I hit on him... He didn't hit on me." *At least, not that night.*

"Hmm..."

"Hmm what, Linda?"

"How many married guys would turn down someone who looked like you?"

"Linda, he was *not* married."

"Hey, I'm just saying you need to figure out those things up front. Look what happened to Debbie last year. Dated that guy for a couple months."

"Oh, I forgot about that. She ran into him at Toys-R-Us when she was shopping for her nephew's birthday."

"Exactly. She had no clue he was married. But there he was with his pregnant wife and their little girl, shopping for tricycles. He was damn lucky she didn't expose him for what a cheating lying creep he was."

"I don't think I'm going to run into Brandon in the toy section with his pregnant wife."

"No, but you need to be careful before you give your heart to some guy."

"I haven't given Brandon my heart."

"Well, you've given him something."

"Oh… shut up."

WHEN FRIDAY ROLLED AROUND AGAIN, SUSAN HAD NOT yet heard from Brandon. Feeling like an anxious high school girl with a new crush, she hung around her apartment all weekend, hoping he would stop by since he didn't have her phone number. He didn't.

The following weekend, she found herself cruising by After Sundown's parking lot, but she didn't see Brandon's red pickup truck. Had she seen it she wouldn't have stopped—but she would have taken it to mean their encounter had definitely been nothing more than a one-night stand to him. If she was brutally honest with herself, she couldn't fault him. After all, she had thrown herself at him, and he had made no promises. Well, he had made one promise. He said he would call, which was an empty promise since he didn't have her number.

Four Saturdays after finding Brandon's note on her pillow, Susan went shopping with her mother and sister. She'd finally accepted the fact Brandon was not interested in her, and she was no longer waiting for him to show up on her doorstep.

Their final stop was the grocery store to pick up last minute items for dinner. Susan's birthday was in a few days, and her mother was preparing an early birthday dinner for her that evening. Susan opted to wait in the car as her mother and sister went into the store. Her mother left the driver's window down so she could get some fresh air.

Alone in the back seat of her mother's vehicle, sitting on the driver's side, Susan's heart seemed to stop when a red pickup truck pulled into a space to the left of her mother's car. An empty parking space separated Brandon's truck and Susan's mother's vehicle.

Speechless, Susan watched as Brandon got out of the truck. For a moment, she thought he had seen her because he walked toward the passenger side of the truck where her mother's car was parked. To her surprise, he turned his back to her and opened the passenger door of the truck, revealing a car seat with a small child.

Scooting down, wanting to disappear, Susan's eyes remained fixed on the car seat while her left hand partially shielded her face. She watched as Brandon lifted a blonde little girl from the truck, setting the child on her feet in the parking lot.

The little girl looked directly at Susan—through blue eyes identical to Brandon's. Even her face was a girlish miniature of Brandon's.

"Daddy," the child said, looking up at Brandon her arms outstretched.

"You want me to carry you, Sarah? Okay, it would probably be faster. We don't want to be late for the dinner your mommy is fixing us!"

Brandon lifted the child up in his arms and gave her a little kiss before shutting his truck door and making his way to the grocery store. He never noticed Susan sitting in the nearby vehicle.

Oh my god. Susan felt sick. Closing her eyes, she covered her face with her open palms. Shame washed over her. *I've slept with a married man! I threw myself at another woman's husband! I'm no better than*

Loretta! No, I am worse... Brandon and his wife have a child!

"Mom, remember when you said I could stay with you and Dad for a while in your spare bedroom?" Susan asked an hour later, as she watched her mother prepare dinner.

"Sure, honey. Isn't your apartment working out?"

"It's just that I made a decision today."

"What kind of decision?"

"I'm really sick of my job."

"I know you said you were going to start looking for a new one when school's out."

"I sort of need to get away for a while. I was thinking about giving Carol a call, see if they need any help this summer at the camp."

"What about your apartment?"

"That's why I asked about staying here. When I moved into my apartment, my neighbor mentioned her sister was going to rent my unit, but I had already signed the lease. I know she hasn't gotten anything yet, so I'm pretty sure she'd take over my lease with no problem. If I stay at the apartment until summer, I may not get anyone to take it over, and I won't be able to get out of it until next November unless I want to lose my deposit. If I'm not tied down to an apartment, I can spend the summer up at Shipley."

"Spend the summer at Camp Shipley? Are you sure you want to do that?"

"Yes, I do. It's a good place to get a fresh perspective on life."

By the following weekend, Susan had moved out of her apartment and was staying at her parents'. She never told Linda what she had learned about Brandon—she felt too foolish. She didn't need her friends to know she'd once again picked the wrong guy. Instead, she led Linda to believe she'd made the decision to cool it with Brandon—that he just wasn't what she was looking for.

Susan felt compelled to sever all imaginary ties to Brandon—which was one reason she wanted to move out of her apartment. While she didn't think he was going to come looking for her, she would prefer he not be able to find her if he did. She took comfort in the fact that John had moved to Texas, thus severing that connection.

A week after she moved into her parents' house, Susan passed Brandon's red truck on the road. Her stomach did a little flip flop when she realized whom she had just passed. Glancing up in her rearview mirror, she let out a little gasp when Brandon made a hasty U-turn and was now driving in her direction. She wasn't certain, but it appeared he had recognized her car and for some reason wanted to catch up to her.

Without thought, Susan made a right turn, and then another, in an attempt to lose Brandon. When she spied his truck driving down the other street, it confirmed her suspicion that he was trying to catch up to her.

"YOU BOUGHT A NEW CAR?" HER FATHER ASKED LATER that night when Susan returned to her parents' home.

"It's my birthday present to myself."

"It's great to have you here," Carol Martin told Susan, who sat across the desk from her in the cluttered log cabin office at Camp Shipley. A cool breeze made its way into the open window behind Susan, filling the room with the scent of pine.

"I'm just glad you had a place for me. I was afraid you'd already be fully staffed for the summer, but I just figured I'd give it a shot." Susan glanced around the office. It had been six years since she'd worked at Camp Shipley, yet little had changed. Even Carol looked just as Susan remembered; she never seemed to age.

"Like I mentioned on the phone, one of the counselors cancelled at the last minute—some family emergency. I was glad you called. But I was sorry to hear about you and Sam."

Susan shrugged and then said, "I suppose it's for the best. I'm just ready to move on."

"Move on? Can I ask you something, Susan?"

"Sure."

"Now, don't take this wrong. I'm thrilled to have you back, but returning to your old summer job that you had back in college. I was wondering why you'd want to return if you say you're moving on."

"Still my old counselor, Carol?" Susan chuckled.

"Some habits are hard to kick. You mentioned on the phone you gave notice at your school district job."

"Yes, I thought it was about time I figured out what I want to do with my life. I never intended to stay at the school district that long. I suppose I just got comfortable there. I had summers off with Sam— with his job, it was convenient. Seemed perfect at the time."

"So why come back here for the summer if you plan to move forward and find a new job? I would think you'd be out pounding the pavement."

"Isn't that obvious? I don't know *what* I want to do. I need to regroup, take a breather. This place was always good for putting life in perspective."

"I guess I can understand that. Your indecision is Camp Shipley's gain." Carol opened her desk file drawer and pulled out a folder. She reached across the oak desk and handed it to Susan.

"These are your girls," Carol explained.

"Still six girls to a cabin?" Susan asked as she took the folder and opened it.

"Yes. You'll be in Cabin Five this summer."

"Fourteen-year-olds," Susan commented as she shuffled through the papers in the file, learning a bit about the six girls assigned to her care.

"All veterans but two. Elizabeth and Kate—this is their first summer."

"How do the four veterans get along?"

"To be honest, I was tempted to break them up."

"What do you mean?" Susan closed the folder and set it on her lap as she looked at Carol.

"Don't get me wrong, they're good girls and fast friends. But remember Claudia and Rachel, back when you went to camp here—before you started working with us?"

"Claudia and Rachel—oh, *yes*. Who could forget? They were here two summers. What a blast. Those girls came up with the most outrageous pranks. My favorite was when they got us to sneak over to the church camp and tip the bell upside down and fill it with water. It was priceless when that guy, all dressed in silk robes, went to ring the bell and got drenched." Susan laughed at the memory.

"Yes, I can see how that would be funny for a fourteen-year-old—but it also caused a camp rivalry that continues today."

"So, what has that to do with the four girls assigned to me?"

"Let's just say they have real Claudia and Rachel potential. Of course, that was last year. Yet, I'm afraid if I break them up, they'll simply commandeer their new roomies to join in their antics. I can also foresee a competition if the four are separated, each trying to see if their cabin of bunkmates can outdo their friends."

"So you want to keep them together and dump them all on me?" Susan chuckled.

Carol flashed a smile and said, "Something like that. But, like I said, they're good girls."

"Hmm…" Susan opened the folder again and shuffled through the pages it contained. "It says here one of the girls caused a dorm fire at her last camp and was sent home."

"That would be Lexi, Lexi Beaumont. She's a sweet girl."

"Carol, are you going soft? Since when do pyro tendencies get a pass from you?"

"Lexi started coming to us the following summer; she was eleven back then. Her grandfather is Ethan Beaumont."

"*The* Ethan Beaumont?" Susan arched her brow.

"The very one."

"So you couldn't turn away all that money?" Susan asked with a chuckle.

"It had nothing to do with his money."

"I was just teasing."

"Lexi's parents were killed when she was ten, and she went to live with her grandfather. The fire incident happened that first summer after her parents were killed. One of the counselors from that camp used to work for us—she gave me a call, wanted to give me the heads up about Lexi because she'd recommended Camp Shipley to Lexi's grandfather."

"I don't understand."

"Apparently Lexi was pretty withdrawn that first summer, getting over the shock of losing her parents and moving in with a man she didn't know."

"She didn't know her grandfather?"

"No. Ethan Beaumont was estranged from his son —her father. A lot of that was in the paper back when he was going for custody. I remember reading about it. The first time she met him was after her parents were killed in the accident. He shipped her off that first summer, and I'm afraid he didn't really check out the camp very well. Lots of rich kids—spoiled rich kids—and Lexi didn't fit in."

"So what happened with the fire?"

"Some sort of a prank the other kids played on her. Technically speaking, she started the fire but it was an accident, and no one was hurt, but she caught the blame since no one wanted to cross the other kids involved because of who their parents were—the camp sent her home."

"Yes, but her grandfather is Ethan Beaumont."

"True. But when he dropped her off at camp, he made it very clear that she was not to get special treatment, and when the incident happened, he never took the time to get Lexi's side. That's why my friend called me and went out of her way to suggest our camp. I guess she tried to talk to Beaumont on behalf of Lexi, but he wasn't interested. She figured Lexi would be happier someplace like Camp Shipley, so she didn't pursue it with her employer."

"How did Lexi fit in here the first summer?"

"She didn't have a problem. Of course, we don't put up with the hazing crap, so she didn't have to endure that here like at the first camp. Lexi is a resilient kid. Not the type to hold grudges. She's more of a problem solver. Self-reliant."

"And the other girls?"

"Barbara's been coming here the longest. First summer was a couple years before Lexi. Like Lexi, she's being raised by a grandparent—more accurately—*grandparents*. Her mother's a drug addict, in and out of jail, and her father has never been in the picture. Last summer, she was pretty boy crazy."

"Boy crazy at thirteen? Look out."

"Colleen's been coming here for two summers. A bright kid. Comes from a pretty conservative Christian family. I was a little surprised they chose us instead of the church camp. The fourth of the *veterans* is Andrea. I think she and Lexi originally bonded from their love of horses. Like Colleen, she's being raised in a home with both her parents. But I get the impression the parents fight a great deal. I haven't met Elizabeth and Kate, your two new girls. Elizabeth is also being raised by both her parents, and she has an older brother. This is her first year at camp. Kate's being raised by her father—and Camp Shipley is her fifth summer camp. Yet, there is nothing in her record that indicates she was ever a problem at the other camps."

"Sound like I'll have my hands full."

"As you know, we keep the girls pretty busy, so you'll have plenty of free time during the day. Time to figure out what you want to be when you grow up."

"Maybe I just won't grow up." Susan grinned.

"It is great seeing you again, Susan."

"What do you mean?" Susan said with a smile. "I see you just about every day on MySpace."

"There is that. How do you feel about leaving your computer back home?"

"I'm okay being unplugged. I don't really go online that often. I take it you still don't have Internet up here?"

"No."

"When I arrived, I tried calling mom on my cell phone to let her know I got here okay."

"Still no cell service on the mountain either."

"I figured that out. I ended up using the payphone in the front."

"How are your folks?"

"Doing great. Mom says hi, by the way." Susan's mother and Carol had been friends since their college years.

"I need to give her a call. Here, let me get you your cabin keys."

"The girls start arriving tomorrow?"

"In the afternoon. It'll be a busy Saturday. I imagine all your girls should be here by Sunday." Carol handed Susan a set of keys from her desk.

"Thanks Carol."

"There'll also be an orientation in the morning for all the counselors before the girls start arriving. You'll want to be at the dining hall at nine in the morning."

"I didn't see anyone when I arrived. Many here yet?"

"Some of the counselors have already checked in. A group of them went down to the village to get something to eat."

"I didn't imagine the mess hall would be open yet, so I brought some food with me."

"Go settle in. You know the routine. Nothing much has changed."

"Thanks again, Carol. I'm happy to be here."

"We're happy to have you. When you're done reading through the folder, please bring it back to my office. I don't like those types of folders floating around when the girls get here."

"No problem. Thanks for having me back."

Carol stood up and walked Susan to the door.

"Will I know anyone in the staff this year?" Susan asked as the two walked outside.

"You won't know any of the counselors. Wait, I take that back. I think a couple were campers here when you worked for us."

"So, basically you're saying I'll be the oldest counselor here?" Susan already knew the answer.

"Pretty much."

"And the dining hall?"

"You'll recognize a couple faces. But you know how it is here; it tends to be a seasonal job for college students. I'm the only constant."

Fifteen minutes later, Susan stood in the camp parking lot removing luggage from her car's trunk. She paused a moment and looked around, breathing in the fragrant mountain air. She guessed it was around seventy-two degrees. The afternoon sun was shining, partially blocked by stately evergreen trees. What sky she could see was blue and free of clouds. The only sounds were from the birds chirping nearby, an occasional rustle of a squirrel scampering up a nearby tree, or a pinecone falling to the ground. She knew it would be much noisier tomorrow when the girls started to arrive.

The camp looked just as she remembered—a

collection of small log cabins surrounded by mature pine trees. Some of her best memories had been made at Camp Shipley, first as a camp guest and later as a camp counselor. This was a safe place for her; it felt like home yet gave her the distance she needed from her everyday life so that she could figure out what road to take when summer came to an end.

CHAPTER NINE

It was late afternoon by the time Susan settled into Cabin Five. Like most of the other guest cabins, furnishing included a picnic table with bench seats, three dressers, three sets of bunk beds for the girls and a full-sized bed with built in drawers for her, the cabin counselor. The cabin also boasted a worn couch, two leather chairs and an oak coffee table. Accommodations were comfortable but not luxurious.

Since the mess hall would not start serving food until the next morning, Susan had come prepared. Two suitcases weren't the only thing she rolled into the cabin—there was also an ice chest filled with sandwiches, snacks, fresh fruit, and beverages.

After unpacking, Susan grabbed a sandwich and bottle of water from her ice chest and set out for a walk. She headed toward the lake and away from the camp's grounds. On route, she passed a number of privately owned cabins. No one lived year round on Shipley Mountain, although some locals lived full-time in the small village at the base of the mountain. Privately owned cabins at higher elevations were used as vacation homes or seasonal rental properties by their owners.

It had been over six years since Susan had been up to Shipley Mountain. During her marriage, she'd tried to talk Sam into renting a weekend cabin up at Shipley, but he had never been interested. He'd had no desire in sharing a nostalgic getaway with his then wife. As she made her leisurely walk toward the lake, she paused in front of a familiar cabin. Smiling, she read the worn wooden sign affixed to the front of it: *Lewis and Clark, minus Clark.*

"I guess that answers my question," Susan said aloud. She had wondered if the Lewises still owned their cabin on the mountain. She didn't see any cars in the driveway, so she assumed they weren't up for the weekend, but then the front door opened, and a young blonde woman walked outside.

Dressed in jeans and a flannel shirt, the blonde woman didn't notice Susan standing along the road beyond the split rail fence encircling her cabin. She kept glancing back at her front door while walking down the driveway.

"Connie? Connie Lewis!" Susan called out when the woman was within hearing distance. The blonde paused a moment, glanced toward Susan and cocked her head slightly as if trying to figure out a puzzle. She then started walking toward Susan.

"Connie will be out in a minute. Do I know you?" the blonde asked.

"Oh my god, it's Ella! You look just like your sister!" Susan said excitedly.

"I remember you!" Ella said with a smile. "You're… Susan, right? You were a counselor at Camp Shipley—a friend of Connie's."

"That's right. You were in high school back then," Susan said with a smile. "I can't believe how much you look like your sister."

"Yeah, I get that a lot. I prefer to say Connie looks like me, but whenever I mention that, she points out she was born first."

"So, what are you doing these days?" Susan asked.

"This time next year I'll officially be a college graduate—assuming of course I pass all my courses."

"Congratulations. What's your major?" Susan asked.

"History."

"History? Impressive. What do you plan to do after graduation?"

"I have absolutely no idea," Ella confessed. They both laughed.

"Are you spending the summer up here? Kicking back until you head back to college?"

"Yes and no. I am spending the summer up here—but I got a summer job at Camp Shipley."

"No kidding! You're a counselor?"

"Lord no," Ella laughed. "I'm working in the mess hall. Something mindless."

"I can relate to mindless."

"What's up with you? Do you have a cabin up here now?" Ella asked.

"No, I'm working at the camp… again."

"Really? I thought Connie said you got married or something."

"Yeah, well… I got divorced this past year."

"Oh, I'm sorry to hear that."

Susan shrugged. "It happens. How's your sister? What's she up to?"

"You can ask her yourself—if she ever gets her butt out here. We were going to walk down to the lake. You're welcome to join us. I don't know what's taking her so long."

"Has she gotten married yet? I haven't heard from her in a couple years."

"Connie? No, she doesn't even have a boyfriend anymore. They broke up a few months ago."

Susan was tempted to say, *There seems to be a lot of that going on*, but resisted. In the next moment, the front door to the cabin opened, and out walked Ella's older sister, who was a few years younger than Susan.

When Connie reached the end of the driveway a

few moments later, she immediately recognized Susan. Hugs were exchanged, and after rapidly recapping recent events in their lives, the three young women decided to walk toward the lake. On route, Susan finished her sandwich as the three chatted.

"Have you started dating again?" Connie asked.

Ella laughed and said, "That is my sister—just comes right out there with the personal questions."

"Oh, that's okay," Susan said with a smile as she glanced over at Connie, who looked not a bit contrite for asking the question but waited anxiously for an answer. "I went out a couple of times, but I haven't really met anyone who sparked my interest."

"I know what you mean. Since Steve and I broke up, I just haven't found anyone who interests me. That was until I saw who rented the cabin next door."

"A cute guy next door?" Susan asked with a grin.

"Yes, cute and *married*," Ella said dryly.

"That sorta killed the deal," Connie said with a sigh.

"A cheating married man—not good," Susan said, thinking immediately of Brandon.

"Oh, I have no idea if he was prone to cheating. But he was a bit of a flirt. Cute as hell."

"He was a bum," Ella chimed in.

"Wow, Ella, it doesn't seem like you have a very high opinion of him."

"Ella doesn't even know him," Connie said.

"I just didn't appreciate how he was all flirty with Connie at the market in the village," Ella explained, ignoring her sister's comment. "And then later, we run into him again, this time as he and his wife and little girl are moving into the cabin next door. Guys like that are scum in my opinion."

"What did he say when he saw you later?" Ella asked.

"I don't think he saw us," Connie said with a shrug. "And, Ella, some guys just flirt. Doesn't mean they're actually going to cheat on their wives."

"There should be a law about wearing a wedding ring," Ella snapped.

"Wow, his being married seems to have upset you more than Connie," Susan noted. When Ella stopped walking for a moment and glared at her, Susan wished she could take back the remark.

"Please, I had zero interest in the bum, if that's what you meant. I just don't like people who don't consider how their actions can affect others." Ella gave a shrug, and then started walking again, picking up her pace and leaving Connie and Susan behind as she made her way to the lake alone.

"I didn't mean to piss her off," Susan said.

"Don't mind Ella. She really was more pissed about him being married and flirting with me than I was. Ella is... well... *principled.* She's okay; don't worry about it. She'll cool down by the time we reach the lake."

"Is she always like that?"

"Ella has always had a low tolerance for bullshit, and as far as she's concerned, a married guy cheating on his wife—or even flirting—is bullshit."

"Then she would have loved Sam," Susan said with a snort.

"I am sorry about you and Sam."

"Thanks. But I'm okay. Honest. And I feel bad about pissing off Ella."

"Don't worry about it. I remember when Ella was still in high school. She was popular enough but never hung out with the jock crowd. There was this guy—captain of the football team who was a major ass. I don't know if he was born that way or simply couldn't handle the fact he was very good looking—he really was—and that all the cheerleaders worshiped him, but he was really into himself. Not a trait Ella adores. I was with Ella at some fundraiser for her school when he came up to her and asked her out. I felt sorry for the guy. He expected her to accept. It was not pretty."

"Not pretty how?"

"He said some nasty things about her later, insinuating her moral character was… lacking."

"What did Ella do?"

"Not what he expected. He and his family went to the same church as one of her best friends, Annie, so Ella asked Annie if she could go to church with her one Sunday."

"This doesn't sound good," Susan chuckled.

"No, but it was funny," Connie giggled. "After church that Sunday, Ella waited until she saw this boy and his parents talking to the minister. Ella marched right up to the minister, and said, 'I think you might want to give your parishioner here some guidance and explain to him that Jesus would not find it amusing to spread lies about a girl simply because the girl refused to go out with him.' She then turned to his parents and said, 'While you might be annoyed at me for embarrassing your son, just imagine how I felt when your son told our fellow classmates that I had been screwing the entire football team. Not only have I never gone out with anyone from the football team—nor would I want to, considering your son's behavior—I do not screw around.' Then she just turned and walked away, leaving the parents and minister speechless."

"What happened?"

"Annie knew the minister—her family had been attending that church all her life. She had no idea what Ella was going to do, but she was aware of the lies he had spread. She was standing there when Ella turned and walked away. Actually, Ella never told me what was said—Annie did. Anyway, according to Annie, she was just as speechless as the other people, but before she went to catch up with Ella, she told the minister—and the parents who were standing there dazed—that it was all true. That he had spread those lies."

"Were the parents pissed at Ella?"

"Surprisingly, no. The next Monday at school, the boy stood up during lunch, told everyone within hearing distance that he owed Ella an apology. She hadn't done those things, and he admitted he had lied."

"That's great. I could see how that might have blown up in her face."

"Funny thing, they actually became friends after that."

"Did they ever date?"

"No!" Connie laughed at the thought. "She accepted his apology and didn't hold a grudge. But ever date him? No. Although, I think he harbored a secret crush on her for years."

"I suppose some guys just want to be smacked." Susan chuckled.

"I guess so... Oh, look... it's him!" Connie stopped walking and reached out, grabbing Susan's wrist. Susan looked toward the lake where Connie was staring. Coming toward her was a blond man carrying a small child. A short distance beyond him was Ella, who stood with her back to the lake watching the man walk toward Susan and Connie. He was busy talking to the child in his arms and didn't notice the two women standing together along the side of the road. When he was about fifteen feet away, he glanced up and saw them. He came to an abrupt stop.

Susan's eyes widened. She couldn't believe what she was seeing. It was Brandon. He looked just as surprised to see her—glancing frantically from the pretty blonde woman he'd recently flirted with to the irritated divorcee whom he had once bedded.

"Enjoying our weather?" Connie said cheerfully. "I see you moved into the cabin next door."

"Umm… yes… we are enjoying our stay," he stammered.

"Have a nice evening," Connie chirped, then slipped her arm through Susan's, tugging her along as they walked toward the lake, leaving Brandon alone with his young charge.

"That is the married flirt I was telling you about," Connie whispered when they were out of earshot.

"Umm..yes…. I sort of figured that out." Still walking arm and arm with Connie, she glanced back over her shoulder. Brandon was still standing at the side of the road with the little girl squirming in his arms as he stared in her direction. Their eyes met.

Curtains from the open window fluttered inward, brushing against Susan's forehead. Restless and trying to get comfortable in the double bed, she turned to one side and clutched the pillow tightly to her belly, before tucking it between her thighs.

The girls wouldn't be arriving until the next day, so she was alone in Cabin Five. She heard a rustling sound—someone was removing the window screen. Holding her breath, she considered screaming, but who would hear her? The closest cabins were empty; their counselors would not be arriving until the morning.

Whoever removed the screen dropped it and was now climbing into the window. The mattress dipped as the person breaking in stepped onto her bed. A second foot hit the mattress. Unable to move, Susan continued to cling to the pillow when the person pulled back the sheets and climbed in the bed with her. It was a man; she could feel his nude body pressing against hers, his erection touching her bottom. Confused, Susan was sure she'd worn a nightgown to bed but now she was nude. Instead of being afraid, she welcomed his uninvited attention.

"Waiting for me Susan?" Brandon's voice whispered in her ear as he wrapped his arms around her, slipping his hands between her body and the pillow, cupping her left breast possessively.

"You're married." The beating of her heart accelerated.

"It's okay; she doesn't know I'm here. She doesn't need to know."

"I can't do this if you're married," Susan told him, yet she did not try to pull away.

"You knew I'd be here, didn't you Susan? You came here looking for me."

"That's not true! I had no idea you'd be here!"

"You're lying. You don't seem surprised I'm in your bed. You didn't scream. You know I'm married, but you still want me, don't you?"

Susan rolled over toward Brandon and wrapped her legs around his hips, holding him like she'd been holding her pillow.

"I do want you, Brandon."

"You're just as bad as Loretta."

"Please don't say that."

"I bet you like it the same way as Loretta did."

Susan was on her hands and knees. She wasn't sure how she had gotten in that position but she didn't have time to think about it because she felt Brandon take a firm hold of her hips. She looked over her shoulder but instead of Brandon, it was Sam, who was laughing. Confused, Susan looked across the cabin and saw Brandon, who was now sitting on a bunk bed with Loretta. The two shared a bowl of popcorn and watched her and Sam. Susan tried to crawl away, but Sam grabbed her and rolled her on her back before climbing atop her body.

Looking up at the man holding her down, Susan saw it was now Brandon—not Sam—and felt a surge of relief.

"It's me you want, isn't it?" Brandon whispered. He was the sweet Brandon she remembered, the one she had known before she'd learned of a wife or child.

"Yes," she whispered, unable to lie.

"Then please, make love to me. I won't tell anyone. No one has to know."

Susan glanced over his shoulder. Sam and Loretta were gone.

"I waited for you to call," she whispered, kissing his lips.

"I know. But I couldn't. I wanted to, but I couldn't." Tenderly he returned her kisses.

"We can't do this," Susan pleaded while caressing his face with her fingertips.

"No one has to know. This will be our secret. I'll come to you every night. Leave your window open when you go to bed."

"I can't. The girls will be here tomorrow."

"They'll be asleep when I come to you. Now, open up for me Susan."

Obediently, Susan wrapped her legs around Brandon's hips and guided him into her body. She couldn't seem to get enough—whatever satisfaction she craved was just around the corner out of her reach. The bed shook as their bodies slammed together in a frantic fury—rushing to some elusive conclusion.

Before Susan could find her release, Loretta and Sam rushed back into the cabin. Now wearing umpire uniforms, the pair jumped up and down while they each blew on a whistle. They wouldn't stop blowing the annoying whistles, so Susan put a pillow over her head trying to block the sound.

The insistent whistling wouldn't stop. Finally, Susan opened her eyes. She was alone in Cabin Five. The alarm clock on the nightstand blared loudly. Disoriented and sleepy, Susan sat up and looked around.

There was no window over her bed; it was on the other wall.

"Bizarre dream," Susan muttered as she turned

off the alarm and climbed out of the bed. Still wearing her nightgown, she stumbled groggily to the bathroom.

By the time she got out of the shower and finished dressing, it was almost 8:00 a.m. After grabbing a carton of yogurt from her ice chest, she went outside. Sitting on the rustic swing on the cabin's front porch, she breathed in the fresh scent of pine as she opened her carton of yogurt and dipped her spoon in for her first bite.

"Good morning," came a nearby voice.

Susan looked up. It was Ella Lewis, standing on the pathway leading to her cabin.

"Ella… hi."

"I've been wandering around for the last half hour looking for someone to ask where I might find you." Ella walked up the porch step to Susan.

"You wanted to talk to me?" Susan pointed to an empty patio chair. Ella sat down.

"I wanted to apologize."

"Apologize, for what? Umm… you want one?" Susan nodded at the yogurt carton.

"No thanks; I already ate. Apologize for being such a jerk yesterday. I'm sorry I was so rude."

"Rude? You weren't rude."

"Yeah… yeah I was. Connie was pretty pissed at me for walking off like that and then going home after *he* showed up."

"Well—"

Ella cut her off. "It's just that Connie was devastated over the breakup with Steve. They'd been together for a couple years. She acts like it was a mutual thing, but he really hurt her. When that bum from next door flirted with her down at the village—before we knew he was married—well, Connie kind of perked up. Like she finally realized there would be other guys after Steve. And when I realized he was married, it just pissed me off."

"So you think Connie was interested in him—the guy from next door?"

"No… I mean yes, at the time… but last night, Connie and I had a long talk. She said it was just fun to flirt, that she really didn't care if he was married or not. After all, they only met for a couple of minutes. I was… well… I guess I was… too…"

"Protective?" Susan asked with a smile.

"I suppose. Kinda silly, huh?"

"I think it's sweet."

"Connie also said I was probably too hard on the guy, too."

"How so?"

"She said lots of people flirt. That it's harmless. Connie said the guy probably didn't mean anything by it, and I needed to stop jumping to conclusions."

Susan stopped eating her yogurt and looked down at her lap in silence.

"What is it?" Ella asked with a frown.

"I agree that some people like to flirt, and it can

be harmless… but…" Susan glanced up at Ella.

"What?"

"I didn't say anything to Connie, but I know your neighbor, his name is Brandon."

"You know him? But when he spoke to you and Connie yesterday…"

"Neither of us acknowledged it, I know."

"I don't understand." Ella frowned.

"I didn't know he was married, either. He's in construction—worked with one of my good friend's brother. When I moved out of my house, he offered to help. I didn't know he was married until… until after."

"After he helped you move?" Ella asked.

"Not exactly. We sort of went out. "

"Oh my god, you mean…?"

"Not my proudest moment."

"That scum. What did he say?"

"He never said anything. I never saw him again. He told me he would call and never did."

"How did you find out he was married?" Ella asked.

"I sort of ran into him at the store. He didn't see me—but he was with his daughter."

"How did you know she was his daughter?"

"For starters, she looks like a mini-him, and she called him daddy. And when they started talking about getting back to mommy, who had dinner ready for them, I thought I was going to be sick. So, Ella, your disgust was merited."

"I'm so sorry, Susan. Do you ever feel like telling his wife what kind of a man she's married to?"

"No!" Susan shook her head. "They have a child, and I don't want to be responsible for breaking up their family."

"It isn't your doing. He's the one being unfaithful to his wife."

"Still, I won't do that."

They sat in silence while Susan finished her yogurt.

"I caught my husband cheating on me."

"Mom always says a guy doesn't normally leave his wife unless he has another woman lined up. That is so wrong."

"I walked in on him and her."

"Would you have wanted someone to tell you about her instead of having you find out that way?"

"I don't know. I've wondered about that myself. I learned after the divorce that my good friends never cared for my husband. I think they tried to get me to see the truth about him before I married him, but what do they say—*love is blind*. I'm not sure if I would have believed had someone told me. Perhaps how I found out was best. Sort of like pulling a bandage off a wound."

"Some guys can be real asses."

"So, tell me, have you seen the wife?"

"Yes. She walks every morning—alone. I passed her yesterday and said hi. She just nodded to me, didn't say anything. Not very friendly, but she didn't look happy that day."

"Maybe she knows about her husband. That would make someone unhappy. What does she look like?"

"I guess she's attractive, but doesn't do much with herself. Of course, it might just be because she's kicking back and enjoying the mountain solitude. Wears old denims and baggy shirts, keeps her hair pulled up in a ponytail. And the day I saw her, I think she had been crying. Her eyes were red."

"Crying? I wonder if she does know. Poor thing."

"What I don't get, whenever I see her husband, he seems like a doting father. He also walks every day— but with the little girl, not his wife. I've watched him from my bedroom window. Sound carries, so I can hear how he talks to her. Very sweet and loving. I don't understand men like that. You'd think if they cared so much about their kids they would try to be better to the mother of their children."

"I know when I met Brandon, he seemed so sweet —and caring. After my divorce, my friends let me know that I was too trusting and had poor taste in men. After falling for Brandon and discovering they were right—"

"Falling for Brandon?" Ella interrupted.

"Yeah…" Susan blushed. "I fell for the jerk. He

seemed like everything I was looking for, and after the night we shared, I thought he was genuinely interested in me. But it was all a lie, and my friends were right."

"That sucks. But don't be too hard on yourself. This is his doing, not yours."

"Thanks, Ella." Susan glanced at her watch. "I better get going. I have a meeting in about fifteen minutes."

"Yeah, I need to get to work, too. I guess I'll be seeing you around. Today's my first day—hope I don't poison the camp!" Ella said cheerfully.

"Me, too!"

CHAPTER ELEVEN

Connie Lewis made herself comfortable in the hammock her father had hung that morning between two pine trees in the side yard of her family's cabin. Engrossed in the romance novel, she failed to notice she was no longer alone.

"Hello." The unexpected greeting jerked Connie back to reality. Startled, she abruptly sat up, almost falling from the hammock.

"I'm sorry," Brandon chuckled, reaching out to steady her. "I didn't mean to scare you."

Clutching her book protectively, Connie looked up at the intruder.

"I thought I was alone." Connie sat upright and placed her feet on the ground. "You startled me."

"I'm sorry. I didn't mean to scare you. I saw you sitting here. Until you mentioned we were neighbors when I saw you down at the lake yesterday, I didn't realize this was your cabin."

"You out for another walk?"

"Actually, I was wondering… yesterday, your friend—the one you were walking with—Susan?"

"How do you know her name?" Connie frowned.

"So, that *was* Susan," Brandon murmured, pretending he hadn't recognized her.

"You know Susan?"

"Yes. I wondered if that was her. Is she staying with you?"

"That's odd; Susan didn't mention she knew you."

"Well…it's been a while. It's possible she doesn't remember me." *More possible she doesn't want to remember me,* Brandon told himself.

"Umm, no, Susan isn't staying here."

"She's no longer on Shipley Mountain?" He sounded disappointed.

"I just said she isn't staying here."

"Can you tell me where I can find her?"

Connie just stared at Brandon for a moment. Finally, she asked, "Why?"

"Why? Well… umm… I'd just like to look her up… umm… say hi." When Connie did not respond, Brandon added, "I'm not a psycho stalker or anything, I promise. Susan and I have some mutual friends—we sort of lost track, and I wondered what happened to her."

"Funny, she didn't say anything when we saw you yesterday."

"Like I said, it has been a long time. Umm... I wasn't even sure it was her when I ran into you two on the road."

"Oh... that's true...." Connie considered his request for a moment longer and then smile. "Susan is working over at Camp Shipley."

"Camp Shipley?"

"It's a girls' summer camp, not too far from here. Susan has a job there this summer as a camp counselor."

"I knew she had the summers off from the elementary school—I didn't realize she planned to work up here."

"Oh, you do know Susan." Connie grinned.

"You thought I was lying?" Brandon was more amused than insulted.

"I wasn't sure. If you plan to look her up, I imagine she's pretty busy today. The campers start arriving this weekend. My sister works there, too."

"Thanks. I appreciate the information. I'll let you get back to your book."

"YOU TOLD HIM WHERE SHE WAS STAYING?" ELLA ASKED Connie when she got home from work late Saturday afternoon.

"He asked if she was staying here. He said they were friends and had lost touch." Connie stood by her easel on the back porch, paintbrush in hand, as she studied the canvas she'd been working on the last two hours.

"Don't you think it was odd Susan didn't mention she knew Brandon when you ran into him yesterday?"

Connie turned from the canvas and looked at her sister. "His name is Brandon?"

"Yes, Susan told me."

"So she did know him!" Connie said with a smile and then turned back to her painting. "What's the big deal?"

"Because she obviously is not interested in seeing him again, which is why she pretended not to know him yesterday."

"I don't understand. Why didn't she say anything to me if she recognized him?"

"You'll have to ask Susan that. But I wish you wouldn't have told him where she was staying until you asked her."

"I think you're making too much of this, Ella. Anyway, I told him she would be too busy to see him today, with the girls checking in. When you see her tomorrow, give her the heads up."

"Connie, why would you give a married man information on where to find one of your friends?"

"Ella..." Connie let out a little sigh. "I told you,

just because he seemed overly friendly in the village doesn't mean he was trying to start something with me. As far as we know, Susan is friends with him and his wife. He certainly didn't try to get friendly with me today. In fact… he didn't even mention his name when he was here." Connie gave a little frown at the thought but then shrugged and went back to her painting, ignoring her sister's concern.

"I DIDN'T EXPECT TO SEE YOU AGAIN TODAY," SUSAN greeted Ella later that evening. She sat on the front porch of Cabin Five.

"You alone?" Ella asked as she took a seat on one of the porch steps.

"My girls are inside the cabin—plotting, I think." Susan laughed. "So, what brings you back here?"

"I just wanted to let you know Brandon came by our cabin today and asked Connie about you."

"What did he ask?"

"He wanted to know where you were staying. He told Connie you were old friends—had lost touch—and that he wasn't sure it was you when you ran into each other yesterday. That of course made sense to my sister since you didn't seem to recognize him. She told him where you were."

"I wonder why he wanted to know."

"He first asked if you were staying with us at the cabin."

Susan thought a moment and then smiled. "Ahh, well that makes more sense. He was probably nervous that I was next door... which, of course, could complicate his life. I imagine he feels better knowing I'm here and not staying so close to his cabin."

"So you don't think he'll look you up like he told Connie?"

"No, I don't think so."

"Okay, I just thought you should know."

"Thanks, Ella, I appreciate it. Did you tell Connie... about Brandon and me?"

"No. I didn't think it was my place to tell her."

"I appreciate that, Ella. When I see Connie again, maybe I'll tell her... I don't know..."

"Susan, why did you tell me?"

Susan didn't answer immediately. "I don't know. I guess I needed to tell someone. I haven't told anyone what happened between Brandon and me... until you."

"Sometimes you just need to tell someone." Ella smiled.

The cabin door swung open and a slim teenage girl stepped onto the porch. She wore denim shorts, a t-shirt, and her dark hair pulled up into a high ponytail.

"Hi," she greeted, looking at Ella. "You work in the mess hall, don't you?"

"Yes, I do."

"Lexi, this is Ella… Ella, Lexi. Ella's family has a cabin up here," Susan explained.

"That's cool," Lexi sat on one of the porch chairs. "Do you work up here every summer?"

"No, this is my first time. Figured it was a good excuse to spend the summer here. Beats working back in the city."

"My parents always talked about getting a mountain cabin. I think that would have been cool. I love it up here," Lexi said wistfully.

"If your parents come up for visitor's day, maybe you can convince them to check out some of the cabins that are for sale," Ella suggested.

"My parents were killed a few years ago," Lexi said matter-of-factly.

"Oh my gosh… I'm so sorry… I…" Ella sounded flustered.

"It's okay. You had no way of knowing." Lexi then added in a cheerful tone, "You two know each other a long time?"

"Yes, but Susan was more friends with my older sister, Connie." Ella glanced at her watch then stood up. "I should probably head back to the cabin. It's been a long day."

"Nice to meet you, Ella," Lexi said.

"You, too, Lexi. Catch you later, Susan."

"Thanks, Ella... for everything," Susan said. Ella gave her a little nod then waved goodbye and headed back to her cabin.

"You all settled in?" Susan asked Lexi when they were alone.

"Pretty much. We were wondering if you wanted to go horseback riding with us tomorrow."

"You sure you want me to tag along?"

"Why not? You do ride, don't you?"

"Yes. In fact, I learned to ride at Camp Shipley—my first summer here. I think I was about ten."

"So you used to be one of us, before you started working here?"

"Yep. I loved spending summers here."

"I never really wanted to spend summers at camp," Lexi said. "I hated the first camp my grandfather sent me to. But... well... I like this one."

"How can you not like a place where there's horseback riding?" Susan grinned.

"I had my own horse," Lexi said quietly, no longer sounding as cheerful as she had moments earlier. "That was one reason I didn't want to go to camp—I wanted to stay home so I could ride Cricket."

"Cricket... that was your horse?"

"Yes. My parents bought him for me. He was the best. Some people say horses are dumb—but not Cricket."

"What happened to him?" By the way Lexi spoke, it was obvious she no longer had the horse.

"My grandfather got rid of him. He was teaching me one of his lessons."

"I'm sorry Lexi. I can't imagine getting rid of something like a horse—or dog—any pet—as a lesson."

"Grandfather said it was my punishment. I went to another camp before this one. There was this incident…"

"The fire?"

"Oh, you know." Lexi sounded amused. "Yeah, I imagine they have that in some file about me."

"I just know you got sent home—something about a dorm fire but no details."

"I'll tell you what happened, if you're curious."

"I suppose I am—a little curious."

"The girls at that camp were…just *lovely*. It was the summer right after my parents died, so I was kind of vulnerable, now that I look back. There was this one group of girls—let's just say they felt it was their job to initiate newbies—and if you showed any vulnerability, they piled it on even more. It didn't matter that I was a few years younger than them. And the counselors there, they didn't pay too much attention to what was going on.

"It was a bunch of little things, one piled up atop another, but what finally did it was when they decided to kidnap me, take me into another dorm, and leave me there in the dark. They'd tied me up—but only tight enough that I would eventually get undone—and give them time to get out of the building and turn off the breaker. That was just in case I found a light switch. But they were kind enough to leave me a book of matches—they put it in my pocket and said I could use that instead of a flashlight."

"I don't understand. Why a book of matches?" Susan asked with a frown.

"First you have to understand that before they left me there, they'd been feeding all the younger girls these scary stories. Not just ghosts but making up tales of how girls had been murdered at the camp—gruesome crap like that. As for the matches, imagine being terrified and finding yourself in a strange building, and the only light you have is from a little match. Just as you get a glimpse of light, the match goes out and you have to light another one."

"You must have been terrified."

"I was. And it didn't help that they booby-trapped the room, so things kept popping out at me in the dark. It was quite ingenious of the girls. They thought the whole thing was hilarious, but in my panic, I dropped a lit match on one of the beds. One thing led to another, and if a counselor hadn't noticed all the lights were off at the dorm and come to check on things, I might not be here today."

"That's horrible. And none of the girls were punished?"

"No one wanted to listen to me, and at the time, part of me was happy to get sent home."

"And your grandfather got rid of your horse?"

"Yep." Lexi gave a little shrug. "It's what Grandfather does. I was just grateful Cricket went to a good home."

"I'm so sorry, Lexi." Susan wanted to smack Lexi's grandfather.

"It was a long time ago. I'm okay. I don't imagine Grandfather was thrilled about being stuck with a kid when my parents died. I've just learned how to deal with him. It's not like he beats me or anything. And I figured you might feel better knowing the story of the fire. I don't want you to be stressing that I might burn you down in your sleep." Lexi stood up and started for the cabin door.

Susan laughed. "I wasn't worried."

"Can we count you in for horseback riding?" Lexi asked cheerfully as she opened the door to the cabin.

"Sure, Lexi. I'd love to go."

Lexi flashed Susan a parting grin as she went back inside the cabin to talk to her bunkmates.

I have a lot to be grateful for, Susan thought when she was once again alone. *Maybe my marriage didn't work, but I have a loving family and good friends.*

While new campers continued to arrive on Sunday, all six of Susan's girls showed up on Saturday. She'd agreed to go horseback riding after lunch, but until then, she had some free time while the girls were occupied elsewhere. Seeking a tranquil interlude, Susan took off for a mid-morning walk.

She made her way up a back trail leading to a little chapel situated on a hillside known as Trail's Chapel. It was located on Forest Service land, and no one knew who had built the tiny structure with its steeple roof, stained glass window, and just enough room to fit one church pew. Some went there for the solitude, some sought shelter from the elements, and some, especially teenagers, saw it as a cool place to make out. Susan went for the solitude.

She had just stepped off the main path and was

heading toward Trail's Chapel when she unexpectedly came face to face with Brandon. Like Susan, he was obviously off for a morning hike—alone.

"Susan." Brandon didn't seem surprised to run into her on the trail.

"Hello, Brandon," Susan said coolly. "I wondered if that was you the other day."

"You didn't recognize me?" Brandon sounded surprised.

"Did you recognize me?" Susan asked.

"Yes."

"You didn't say hello."

"It was a little awkward under the circumstance."

"Yes, I imagine it would be. Well, have a nice walk." Susan started on her way again, leaving Brandon standing alone on the trail.

"Susan, wait… We need to talk…"

Susan didn't respond, nor did she stop walking. Brandon let out a little curse when she failed to stop.

"We have nothing to talk about," Susan said when Brandon caught up to her. She was almost at the chapel.

"I'm sorry I didn't say hello the other day," Brandon said.

"Yes, you explained; it was *awkward*. I get it. No problem. Please, I would just like to be alone. I only have a little free time before I have to get back to the camp." Susan paused at the chapel door, waiting for Brandon to leave.

"I just want a couple minutes of your time."

Before she could reply, they heard horseback riders making their way down the trail. Without thought, Brandon grabbed Susan by the arm and pulled her into the chapel.

"What did you do that for?" Susan snapped.

Brandon glanced out the chapel door and watched as the horseback riders rode by. There were at least a dozen. He was relieved when they rode by the chapel without stopping.

"I just wanted to be alone so we could talk," Brandon explained.

Susan wondered briefly if she should be afraid, alone with Brandon in the isolated chapel. If she shouted for help now, the horseback riders would probably hear her, yet she didn't feel as if she were in danger.

"Brandon, we really have nothing to talk about."

"I stopped by your apartment, but they told me you had moved, and no one seemed to know where to."

"Gee, I was there for a good month after the last time I saw you in town."

"I had too much going on. I figured you'd understand—know why I hadn't come by—under the circumstances." Brandon paused a moment and studied Susan's expression, wondering briefly if she *did* understand.

"I didn't right away, but, yes, I know why you didn't come by."

"I was so surprised to see you up here."

"I imagine you were."

"Susan, I'd like to see you again."

"You would? You mean…. maybe I can slip away some night from camp?" Susan wanted to smack him.

"Oh no. I don't think that would be a good idea. Not here."

"You mean your family?" Susan asked sweetly.

"Yes. I promised Kit and Sarah this was family time—under the circumstances. You do understand, right? But I'd like to see you again."

"Are you serious?" Susan used all her willpower to maintain her cool.

"I've thought of you a lot since that night."

"Can I ask you something, Brandon?"

"Sure."

"Did you flirt with Connie in the village? Were you interested in her—like you are interested in me?"

"Connie?" Brandon looked confused.

"Connie—the girl I was walking with when we bumped in to each other. Her cabin is next door to yours."

"I suppose I flirted with her a little. It didn't mean anything. How long are you staying up here?"

"All summer. You?" Susan smiled sweetly, but she wanted to give him a good kick in the groin.

"For most of the summer. I'd love for us to try and get together, but it might be difficult with my family up here."

"Brandon, do me a favor—do all of us a favor—and go back to your family."

Without saying another word, Susan pushed past Brandon and walked back outside.

"Susan!" Brandon called after her. "You seriously aren't upset at me because I have to spend this time with my family?"

Susan stopped walking and turned to face Brandon.

"Absolutely not," Susan said, no longer being sarcastic. "I sincerely think you should spend this time with your family. They need you."

"Yes, they do," Brandon agreed.

"That little girl…"

"You mean Sarah?" Brandon asked.

"Yes. She looks just like you, you know."

"People are always telling me that. But I think she looks just like her mother."

"How old is Sarah?"

"Four."

"She's a beautiful child. I can tell she adores you."

"She's the world to me," Brandon said.

"And her mother?" Susan asked.

"What do you mean?"

"How do you feel about her mother?"

"That's an odd question," Brandon said.

"Is it?"

"I naturally love her. I would think that goes without saying."

Susan just stared at Brandon for a moment. She suddenly remembered what Sam had told her about his affair with Loretta. *I'm sorry, Susan, I never intended to fall in love with her. I just thought it would be a harmless fling.*

She wondered, *Did most married men go around having what they believed were harmless flings?*

"The thing is, Brandon," Susan began, using all her strength to maintain her composure. "I'm simply not interested. The night we shared… it was fun, I guess. But hey, I was horny—hadn't had sex for months. I suppose any guy at After Sundown would have done the trick for me. You scratched my itch—I appreciate the favor—but I've moved on. Sorry, I'm not interested in a repeat performance."

Without another word, Susan turned from Brandon and made her hasty retreat down the path and back to Cabin Five.

CURLED UP IN THE FETAL POSITION IN THE MIDDLE OF her bed, Susan finally stopped crying. She needed to dry her tears before the girls came back from lunch. Her stomach churned—sick not only from Brandon's Sam-like attitude toward marriage and fidelity, but also over the crude words she had spoken, transforming what she once believed had been a beautiful night into something ugly and shameful.

I don't say phrases like scratch my itch, she told herself. Yet she had. Susan cursed herself for trying to wound Brandon's ego when she should have been truthful and told him how she really felt. He needed to know how much he had hurt her—how his actions were hurting his wife and child. Instead, she had led Brandon to believe she condoned his behavior that she might even continue in the adulterous affair if she had found him attractive enough.

"Did you have a nice walk?" Kit asked Brandon when he returned to the cabin later that afternoon.

"I should have taken Sarah fishing instead," he grumbled.

"Sarah's taking a nap." Kit explained in a whisper. "Come; let's go outside so we don't wake her. She's been cranky all morning and needs her sleep."

Silently, Brandon followed Kit outside to the front porch. They sat down together on the porch swing.

"Looks like Sarah isn't the only cranky one. Need a nap, Brandon?" Kit teased.

"Maybe I do," Brandon said with a pout.

"What happened on the walk? You seemed rather anxious when you left. What's up?"

"Nothing." Brandon shrugged. "Nothing, really. The other day, I spotted a woman I know from home. I just wanted to say hi to her. That's all."

"Did you find her?"

"Yes, but I sort of wished I hadn't."

"Why, did something happen?"

"No, nothing happened. It's just that. You know how sometimes when you meet someone and you think they are really a nice person, someone you'd like to get to know, and then you see them again, and they aren't anything like you remember?"

"I suppose. By your attitude, I take it you thought better of her when you first met her, and she didn't quite live up to your memory."

"I guess you could say that."

"Do I know who she is?"

"No, you've never met her."

"Will I ever meet her?"

"I seriously doubt it." Brandon wrapped his arm around Kit's shoulder and pulled her to his side. They sat quietly together in the porch swing while Brandon used one foot to push it to and fro, in a steady rhythm. Kit rested her head on his shoulder and closed her eyes.

As the two sat quietly in the porch swing, they paid little attention to the horseback riders making their way down the street.

Had Susan known the horseback ride would take them down the street where Brandon was staying, she would have made some excuse to skip the ride. But it was too late to do anything about it now, so she said nothing and rode silently with the group as they passed Brandon's cabin.

She felt as if someone had kicked her in the stomach when she spied Brandon sitting on the porch swing with the blonde woman. *It's his wife,* Susan told herself. While she was too far away to get a good look, Susan couldn't miss the way the two cuddled together in the porch swing with Brandon's arm possessively around the woman.

"Brandon," Kit whispered, her eyes still closed. She could hear the horses making their way down the street.

"Yes, Kitty?"

"Thanks for bringing us up here. I needed this. Sarah needed this, too."

"You know I'd do anything for you, Kitty."

"I know, Brandon. You're a good brother."

CHAPTER THIRTEEN

After breakfast on Monday morning, Susan was walking with Lexi and Andrea to the stables when they passed Carol, who was standing at the door of her office talking to a young woman. The woman, who Susan did not recognize was holding the hand of a little girl. When Susan's gaze dropped to the child, there was immediate recognition. It was Sarah—Brandon's daughter.

"Oh, Susan, can you come here for a minute?" Carol called out.

Susan, who had just walked past Carol, stopped in her tracks and took a deep breath, mustered a smile and turned to face the two women and a child. "Yes, Carol?" she asked cheerfully, then turned to Lexi and Andrea and said, "You girls go on. I'll meet you at the stables." Both girls nodded and continued on their way.

"Susan, this is Kit Landon," Carol introduced when Susan walked closer. "Kit, this is Susan Thomas, one of our counselors. In fact, Susan lives in the same town as you do. Perhaps you already know each other."

"No, I don't think so," Susan said nervously.

"Nice to meet you, Susan. They do say it's a small world." Kit smiled.

Susan couldn't help but notice how attractive Kit was despite the fact she wore tattered denims, an oversized flannel shirt, and her blonde hair pulled atop her head in a careless ponytail. But it was the blue eyes that caught her attention, and when she glanced down at the small child, she noticed how much the two looked alike. Brandon was right; Sarah did look just like her mother.

"Susan, I wondered if you would do me a favor."

"Sure, Carol, whatever you need." *Especially if it gets me away from this awkward situation.*

"This is Kit's daughter, Sarah," Carol introduced.

Susan glanced down at the child who was now curiously looking up at her.

"Hello, Sarah," Susan greeted in a soft voice.

"Are you going to show me the horses?" the child asked.

"I was wondering if you would walk Kit and Sarah over to the stables," Carol explained. "I promised Sarah she could see the horses today, but

I'm afraid something came up, and I don't want to disappoint her."

"Carol, if you are busy…" Kit began.

"No, Kit I don't want to disappoint Sarah. I know this means a lot to her."

Kit stopped protesting and smiled down at Sarah. Susan wondered why it was so important—and how did Carol know Kit?

"Umm, sure… I can take them to the stables," Susan said, trying her best to sound cheerful.

"I really appreciate this," Kit told Susan a few minutes later as the three walked toward the stables with Sarah holding her mother's hand.

"Sure, no problem," Susan lied.

"Sarah saw some of the horseback riders the other day, and ever since then, she's been begging me to get a closer look. I told Carol about it, so she suggested I bring Sarah over this morning and meet the horses."

"So, how do you know Carol?" Susan asked, curious.

"We met at a restaurant expo a few years back."

"Restaurant expo?"

"We hit it off immediately and kept in touch ever since. She's the one that arranged the cabin rental for us."

"Umm… yes… I think I noticed you there when I rode by the other day. One of my friends is your neighbor—the Lewis cabin."

"Oh! You mean *Lewis and Clark, minus Clark*?"

"Yes, that one." Susan smiled. "Mr. Lewis thinks that sign is hilarious. Not sure his daughters agree."

"I noticed many of the cabins have cute names."

"Yes. People like to name their cabins, it seems."

"Do you have a cabin up here, too?" Kit asked.

"No. I'm just here for the summer, working as a counselor."

"This is a very peaceful place. I'm glad we came. We needed this time away."

"Here we are," Susan announced the obvious when they reached the stable's gate where Lexi and Andrea waited.

"Girls, this is Mrs. Landon and her daughter Sarah. Sarah would like to meet the horses," Susan explained.

"Girls, please call me Kit."

"Hello, Sarah." Lexi dropped to her knee and greeted the small child.

"Hi, Sarah. You like horses?" Andrea asked, leaning down with her hands propped on her knees as she smiled into the little girl's face.

"Oh, yes!" Sarah squealed.

Lexi put out her hand for Sarah. Before taking it, Sarah looked up at her mother, who gave a little nod. Grinning, Sarah took hold of Lexi's hand and walked with her and Andrea to the corral to meet the horses.

"They seem like nice girls," Kit noted as she

watched the teenagers lead Sarah closer to the corral, chatting all the way.

"Those two know their way around horses. They keep insisting I go riding with them. I'm afraid if this becomes a daily thing, I'll have a problem sitting down before long." Susan chuckled.

"That must mean the girls like you," Kit said.

"I am flattered they asked me to go with them."

Near the corral, Andrea took hold of Sarah's hand while Lexi sprinted back to Kit and Susan.

"I was wondering if I could take her for a ride," Lexi asked. "We'll stay in the corral, I'll have her wear a helmet, and she can sit on my lap. Lady Jane is a real sweet horse, so you don't have to worry."

"She would love that. Do you think it'll be okay? I don't want to do anything that will get you in trouble," Kit said.

"I'll run it past the stable manager first. If it's okay with her, there's no problem," Lexi explained.

Susan silently watched Kit, who was staring at Sarah while trying to make a decision.

"Okay, that would be great," Kit said at last. "Is it okay if I take a picture? I brought my camera."

"If you didn't have one with you, I was going to offer to go get mine," Lexi said with a grin before sprinting back to the corral to tell Sarah the good news.

"That's really nice of them," Kit said, her eyes still focused on her daughter.

Susan and Kit stood in silence as they watched Lexi saddle Lady Jane while Andrea held Sarah's hand and patiently explained to the little girl what Lexi was doing. When Sarah was finally on the horse, sitting in front of Lexi and holding tightly to the saddle's horn, she broke into an excited smile and didn't seem a bit afraid when they started making their way around the corral.

"She reminds me of her father," Kit said after snapping a few pictures, tears filling her eyes. Susan glanced at Kit and noticed the tears.

"She seems to be enjoying herself."

"When I was a little girl, I was such a chicken. No way would I get on a big horse, even with someone else. But Sarah—just like her daddy—is willing to try new things." Kit wiped away the tears that slid down her face. "Excuse me. It seems all I do is cry anymore."

"Sometimes we just need to cry." *That was lame,* Susan told herself after the words left her mouth.

"And sometimes crying is all we can do," Kit said, wiping away more tears.

"I know I cried a lot after my divorce," Susan found herself saying, desperately wanting to help the woman she believed she had wronged.

"You're divorced? Oh, I'm sorry. When I got married I thought it would last forever," Kit said wistfully. "He was my knight in shining armor. But we never know what the future has in store for us, do we?"

"There are no knights in shining armor," Susan countered.

"I think my husband was. If things had been different, I think our marriage could have lasted forever."

Susan eyed Kit curiously. When Kit noticed Susan's inquisitive glance, she blushed.

"I'm sorry. I guess I should explain. My husband was killed in March."

"Killed?" Susan stared at Kit.

"Since we live in the same town, I imagine you heard about it. His name was Kevin Landon—he was a Realtor."

"Oh my god," Susan gasped. "Yes, I did read about it. My ex-husband is a Realtor, and I remember wondering if he knew him. I'm so sorry."

Kit smiled sadly, her eyes still on the riders. "Brandon wanted to get me and Sarah out of the city for a while. He said we needed the break, and I think he was right."

"Brandon?" Susan felt ill again.

"Brandon. He's my baby brother. Although these days, I feel like he's my big brother, the way he's taken care of us. I don't know what I would have done without him. He's been there for me every minute. But, I'm not his responsibility. I've told myself that when we get home I will find some way to stand on my own two feet. Sarah needs me—and Brandon needs to live his own life."

"I am so sorry Kit… I had no idea."

Silently, Susan thought back to her night with Brandon—and the news of Kevin Landon's murder. If she remembered correctly, the murder had happened the morning Brandon had left her house—which would explain why he hadn't tried to contact her. He obviously had other, more important things on his mind.

"How has Sarah been handling all this?" Susan's heart broke for the little girl and Kit.

"She doesn't understand the finality of it all and keeps asking when her daddy is coming home. She's become very attached to Brandon. They were close before, yet I've noticed she's latched onto him since Kevin's death. She went through a period a while back where she started calling Brandon Daddy."

"She doesn't do that anymore?" Susan remembered the first time she'd seen Brandon and Sarah together and how the little girl had called him Daddy, which led her to believe he was the father.

"Once in a while—but no, not really. It bothered Brandon; I think even more than it did me. He pretty much solved the problem by setting aside time for Daddy talks."

"Daddy talks?"

"That's what Brandon calls it. He shows Sarah pictures of Kevin and tells her little stories—like how

Kevin used to have tea parties with her—jogging her memories. And afterwards he asks, *who's your daddy?* And she will always point at the picture of Kevin."

"Wow… that's sweet."

"Yes. My brother is a sweet guy. I keep waiting for him to settle down, but he insists he has no business getting into a serious relationship until he can financially commit."

"Financially commit?" Susan frowned.

"That's what he calls it. Basically, it means he wants to be in the position to ask a woman to marry him if he falls in love, and that means being capable of supporting her."

"Sounds a little old fashioned." Susan couldn't help but think of Sam—he had relied on her for primary support after they married.

"I suppose he is. I am, too. All I ever wanted to do was be the traditional housewife. I know that isn't politically correct these days. Kevin and I agreed I would stay home—raise our children, be there for Kevin when he came home at night after a long day's work. It was a simple dream. One I thought I'd actually obtained. But all that changed in March."

onday afternoon, Susan found Brandon fishing at the lake. It wasn't difficult tracking him down, considering Kit had mentioned her brother planned to take Sarah fishing after lunch. He sat on a fallen log, fishing pole in hand, with his back to Susan. A baseball cap shielded his eyes from the sun, and he hadn't yet noticed Susan's reluctant approach.

Nearby, Sarah sat on the beach, building what appeared to be her version of a sand castle, while her bright pink fishing pole lay forgotten in the dirt. She wore blue overalls with a white t-shirt and sandals. A blue bonnet sat lopsided atop her mop of blonde curls.

According to the outside thermometer affixed to a pole near Cabin Five, it was almost eighty-five degrees. With the light breeze, Susan thought it felt a little cooler by the lake. The only clouds in the blue sky were fluffy white and non-threatening.

Susan stood quietly, trying to muster the courage to make her presence known. After taking a deep breath, she took another step forward, casting a shadow over Brandon.

Startled, he glanced up. Susan stood between him and the bright afternoon sun. She moved to the side slightly. He squinted and then looked back to the lake, to avoid looking directly into the glaring light.

"Hello," she said.

"Hi, Susan! Want to play in the sand with me?" Sarah called out.

"Umm… not right now, honey. I need to talk to your Uncle Brandon."

Sarah smiled and went back to her play. Brandon glanced from Sarah to Susan and then back to the lake. He seemed more interested in fishing than hearing what Susan wanted to say.

"I met your niece and sister today at the camp," Susan explained.

"Yes, I heard," Brandon said dully, his back to Susan. "What do you want?"

"I need to apologize."

"What for?" He reeled in his line. The bait was gone.

"I thought you were married." Susan remained

standing. Brandon didn't appear to be overly interested in what she had to say. Removing a red worm from a carton by his feet, he affixed the wiggly creature onto the hook and cast it back into the water.

"Why would you think that?" He continued to look ahead, away from Susan.

"Well… you said you would call and never did."

"If I remember correctly we forgot to exchange phone numbers. But I did leave the note."

"When you said you'd call?" Susan frowned.

"No. The second note on the following Monday. I put it on your door. Explained why I'd be tied up for a while, left you my number."

"I never got it."

Brandon shrugged as if he didn't quite believe her. "Still doesn't explain why you thought I was married."

"To begin with, I saw you in the grocery store parking lot with Sarah. She called you Daddy."

"Where were you?" He looked up at her briefly, then back to the lake.

"I was in the parked car next to your truck."

"And you didn't say hello?"

"No, I mean, she called you Daddy."

"Some little kids call every man they meet Daddy. And even if she was mine, that wouldn't necessarily mean I'm married."

"I… I just assumed."

"Yeah, I get that. You assumed a lot of crap."

"I'm sorry, Brandon. When I saw you up here with Kit, I thought she was your wife."

"It was in all the papers, Susan. They interviewed me on the news. Even if I hadn't left the note, I find it hard to believe you didn't know what happened."

"I did, but I had no idea it was your brother-in-law."

"So, what was all that bullshit yesterday? Why didn't you just come out and say what was really on your mind? What was with the game playing?"

"Game playing? I wasn't playing games. I was hurt."

"*Hurt?* I don't have time for petty drama queen bullshit." Brandon reeled in his line and tossed his fishing pole to the ground. He looked up at Susan. "I guess I have a low tolerance for game playing these days."

Susan felt as if she had been slapped. She didn't know how to respond.

"You know, Susan," Brandon continued, his voice low so Sarah wouldn't hear. "When I first met you, I really liked you. I liked the fact that when we helped you moved you offered to pay us and didn't come across as a tease who just wanted free help. I liked the fact that you approached me at After Sundown— came right out and said what you wanted. I liked the honesty.

"Since this thing with my sister, I've taken a closer

look at what I want out of life. There's so much we can't control. In an instant, everything can be gone. I thought a lot about you over the last couple months. When you didn't call me right away, I didn't have time to question what that meant. I was pretty wrapped up with Kit.

"In spite of that, I couldn't stop thinking of you, so I went to your apartment again—but you had moved, and no one knew where you'd gone. Later, I saw you driving down the road and I tried to catch up to you—I still wanted to talk to you. But it was pretty obvious to me that you saw my truck. You went out of your way to ditch me."

"I thought you were married…" Susan said.

"Yeah, I get that. So by some strange act of fate we see each other again, and you totally blow me off like you have no clue who I am. I figure the whole thing is damn awkward, so I don't say anything in front of your friend. But I can't stop thinking of you, and figure, if I could just talk to you one more time, I could at least figure out how to get you out of my head."

"Brandon… I thought you were *married*."

"Yes, Susan," Brandon said impatiently. "I said I *get* that. What you said to me yesterday, let's just say it worked. You're out of my head, at least in that way. I'm not sure what I want out of life, but I know what I don't want. I can't waste my time with someone who'd rather jump to conclusions instead of coming right out and asking if there's a problem. Or at least telling me why they're so pissed at me. Look how much bullshit could've been avoided if, when you saw me at the grocery store, you would've simply said, *Hi Brandon, I thought you were going to call me? Oh, and who is the kid?"*

Susan didn't have a response. Nothing made any sense to her. *Why doesn't he understand?* She thought this was going to be easy, that once she explained the misunderstanding, he would accept her explanation, and they could… *They could what?*

"Come on, Sarah. Time to go home," Brandon said as he stood up and gathered his fishing tackle.

"Do we have to?" Sarah asked.

"Yes, Sarah. Your mom is baking some cookies, and I know how you love warm cookies."

Sarah jumped up. "Can Susan go with us?"

"No, sweetie. Susan has to go now. She's a very busy lady."

Susan took a deep breath and willed herself not to cry.

"YOU'RE TELLING ME THE SUSAN I MET THIS MORNING—the one who took Sarah and me to the stables—is who you were talking about, the one who didn't quite measure up?" Kit asked as she dipped her chocolate chip cookie into a glass of cold milk before taking a bite.

"Yes." Brandon sat next to his sister at the breakfast bar in the cabin. In the next room, Sarah had fallen asleep on the sofa.

"She seemed really nice this morning. I guess she's divorced. Did you know her ex?"

"No. But he was a Realtor like Kev."

"Yeah, she mentioned that. So, what's the deal; did you guys date or something?"

"We went out once. I helped her move."

"Don't tell me—you forgot to tie down her dining room table!" Kit teased.

"Ha ha, funny. Nothing flew out of the back of my truck. But she got the impression I was married."

"Married? I don't understand." Kit frowned.

"Apparently, there was a breakdown in communications. We forgot to exchange phone numbers, so I left a note at her apartment, which she claims she didn't get."

"Why would she lie?"

"I'm not saying she lied about it."

"Why did she think you were married?"

"She saw me and Sarah at the store. I didn't see her. It was back when Sarah was calling me Daddy."

"Ahh. Well, Sarah does look enough like you to make that understandable."

"True, but she could've asked. I didn't even know she was there. Instead, she jumps to conclusions."

"Do you know why her marriage ended?"

"From what I understand, her husband had a girl-friend. Apparently, she walked in on them."

"Well gee, Brandon, the poor girl has trust issues."

"Are you taking her side?"

"I'm not taking anyone's side. But cut the girl some slack. Did you… um… you know?"

"Are you asking me to kiss and tell?" Brandon asked.

"I'm not asking for details. I was just curious; it would explain a lot."

"Yeah, we spent the night together. A pretty amazing night…"

"Hey, I said no details!" Kit laughed. "Has she dated much since her divorce?"

"Not really. A little perhaps. But… I guess I was the first person she slept with since the break up."

"That poor thing!"

"Thanks a lot Kitty," Brandon scoffed. "While I don't expect my sister to see me as a sexual object…"

"Ewww, I certainly hope not!" Kit wrinkled her nose.

"I'd just hope she'd give me more credit. Some women—those not related to me of course—think I am quite the guy between the sheets."

Kit laughed and patted Brandon's forearm. "Yes, dear, I'm sure you are. You just aren't much up here." She smacked his head.

"Hey, what was that for?" It didn't really hurt, but it was the principle of the thing.

"Think, Brandon. This woman has just been betrayed by the man she loves. The man she vowed to spend her life with. To make matters worse, she witnessed the betrayal. Now, fast forward in the future. She meets a new guy, and according to you, it was a pretty amazing night. But then later, she discovers he's married—or at least that's what she believes."

"She could have asked me."

"True, Brandon. But maybe she wasn't emotionally equipped to ask. In her mind, she is an adulteress… no different than the woman she caught with her husband."

"I still say she could've asked, I think I deserved the benefit of the doubt."

"Maybe you did, Brandon, but like I said, give her some slack. Why should she have trusted you? Had you earned her trust?"

"Okay, Kit; I sort of get what you're saying. But I just don't need her baggage in my life."

"We all come with baggage, Brandon."

"True. But I want a woman who'll trust me, talk to me. I don't want to go through my life second-guessing what she's really thinking. I don't want the drama."

"I get that, Brandon. But you have to work for those things. And that doesn't mean searching the world for a woman who'll give you blind trust, but finding the woman to build trust with. It's a mutual give and take. I don't think you should accept anyone on face value, and frankly, you're expecting way too much from her after just one date. And I don't care how amazing that one night was."

louds gathered overhead, threatening a summer storm. Grateful for the windbreaker she'd thrown on before leaving the cabin; Susan wrapped her arms around her body and hugged the garment closer. It had reached the upper eighties the day before, yet now, with the cool afternoon breeze, Susan guessed it was in the low seventies.

She couldn't believe it had been a week since she'd arrived—it was Friday again. Since her encounter with Brandon at the lake, she'd avoided walking down Connie's street, not wanting to run into him. It wasn't just that he'd made it perfectly clear he was no longer interested—but he seemed to dislike her.

She'd told Ella why she'd stayed away, which is one reason Connie had showed up after lunch and asked Susan if she wanted to go for a walk. As it turned out, Susan was getting ready to take a hike with the girls from her cabin, so she invited Connie to join them.

The two took their time, trailing behind the younger girls as they chatted. That morning, all eight had opted for denims instead of shorts—it was simply too chilly for beachwear. The breeze sent a gentle movement through the treetops, adding a nip to the air.

"Just what is she going to do with all those pinecones?" Connie asked Susan as the two followed the girls down the mountain trail leading to the back entrance of the stable. Up ahead, Lexi was busy picking up pinecones and putting them in a pillowcase while her cabin mates walked along the trail with her, chatting and pointing out well-formed pinecones.

"I guess she has some deal with a craft store back where she lives. They're buying whatever she brings them, providing the pinecone is in pristine condition," Susan explained. "I think she wanted to grab what she could find, just in case it does rain."

"Is that even legal?" Connie asked with a frown, her eyes still on Lexi.

"She checked with the ranger. He limited where she could collect them, what type, and how many."

"She asked permission? I'm impressed."

"Lexi's a spunky kid. From what I understand,

she's always figuring out some way to make extra cash."

"Didn't you say her grandfather was Ethan Beaumont?"

"Yes, she lives with him; he's her guardian."

"And only heir, from what I've read in the paper," Connie noted. "Part of me wonders why someone like that would bother collecting pinecones to earn a little cash when her family is worth millions. But then, I figure it's probably part of her DNA, like Gramps—looking for ways to make money."

"I don't think it's that," Susan said as she watched Lexi down the trail with her friends.

"What do you mean?" Connie glanced over at Susan and then back down the trail.

"I guess last year Lexi convinced the stables to hire her part time while she was here so she could earn some extra money."

"That sounds odd." Connie frowned. "Her grandfather pays to have her go to camp—and then she takes on a job at the camp?"

"I know. Carol told me about it. She had to put the kibosh on it for insurance reasons—and never told Mr. Beaumont. I guess Lexi begged her not to say anything. From what I gather, her grandfather is not overly generous with his granddaughter, and tight purse strings are a way to control her. The only reason he sends her to camp is to get rid of her."

"Seriously?"

"I have a feeling Lexi is tucking away a bankroll to make her big escape someday."

"Why do you say that?"

"When we go to bed at night, I hear a lot. The girls never go right to sleep. I think they have their deepest conversations after they hit the mattress. Not sure if they think I can't hear them or that I'm asleep, or maybe they just don't care if I overhear what they're talking about."

"Don't you think you should say something to Carol? I mean it sounds like Lexi might be planning to run away."

"No, it's not like that. Apparently, Lexi is determined to go to college, and her grandfather has agreed to pay for that. But after college is another story, and that girl is already arranging her escape plan."

"Don't you think he'll wonder what she's doing with a bag of pinecones?"

"From what I understand, a driver picks her up. It's not like old man Beaumont is waiting to greet his granddaughter when she comes home at the end of summer."

"That's sad. My folks sometimes drive me nuts, but they're always there for Ella and me."

"How does Ella like working at the camp?"

"She hasn't complained. I think she likes it okay. Spends her free time reading. By the way, she mentioned Brandon next door isn't married, that the woman with him is his sister."

"Yes and the little girl is his niece."

"Ella mentioned that was the reason you were reluctant to come over—that you wanted to avoid running into him. But I sorta figured after you found out he was single that you and he… you know… he did look you up. And he is so darn cute."

"I sorta burned that bridge," Susan said as she glanced down and kicked a rock with the toe of her tennis shoe.

"What do you mean?"

"I was pretty bitchy with him the other day when he tried talking to me. The fact I thought he was a cheating husband didn't soften him when I went to apologize, just made him more annoyed. Apparently, he is looking for a woman who doesn't play games— who is more honest."

"Are you serious?" Connie stopped in her tracks and looked at Susan. "You're one of the nicest, most honest, and real people I know! What a jerk!" Connie started walking again.

"Oh, don't be too rough on him. I suppose he had a point. And when I think about it, he's been going through a lot these last few months." Susan tucked her fingertips in the back pockets of her denims as she walked down the trail.

"Ella was telling me about his brother-in-law. He was killed in some sort of holdup."

"It was pretty big news back home. Local Realtor

stops in at a convenience store on his way home to grab a gallon of milk and some drugged-up guy kills him for twenty bucks."

"He was a Realtor? Did Sam know him?"

"I don't think so, maybe. I never discussed it with him."

"I guess you don't talk much to Sam these days."

"Not really. Although, he did ask me to come back with him. As usual, his timing was impeccable. It wasn't long after our divorce was finalized."

"No kidding. Did you … consider it?"

"No, not even for an instant. Which was actually something of a turning point for me."

"How so?"

"It wasn't just that I realized I was totally over him—I realized he was never the person I thought he was."

"What do you mean?"

"For one thing, he wasn't asking me to come back because he suddenly realized he was still in love with me. He'd simply broken up with his girlfriend and needed a place to stay. Plus, I'd just banked my share from the sale from our house, and I think in his mind that money was still his."

"What an ass."

"Yeah, that's pretty much what I thought."

They walked for a few moments in silence when Connie finally said, "I can't stop thinking of Brandon's brother-in-law. That's so senseless."

"It is. I had no idea he was connected to Brandon. And when I saw him with Sarah, well they looked so much alike I just assumed he was her father. I suppose he was right when he told me that I should have simply asked him when I saw them together—instead of hiding and not saying anything."

"I haven't met his sister yet. She keeps to herself," Connie said.

"She was very friendly when she came up to the stables with her little girl."

"What was she doing up there?" Connie asked.

"Her daughter wanted to see the horses, so Carol invited her up. I guess they're friends, Carol and Brandon's sister."

"Small world," Connie noted. "Did she know you knew her brother?

"No, I don't think so. She also looks a lot like her brother, very attractive. Funny thing, when I first met her at the stables, it didn't even dawn on me that they were siblings in spite of how much they looked alike."

"I remember my mother once telling me that when she and Dad were dating in high school, this guy asked them if they were twins, and the creepy thing, they were holding hands at the time!" Connie told her.

"That is bizarre. Not that they looked alike, but that a brother and sister that age would be holding hands."

"I know. A real *Flowers in the Attic* sort of thing." They both laughed.

"What are you doing the rest of the afternoon?" Susan asked.

"I'm heading back to the cabin when we get to the stables. I need to finish that painting. Thanks for inviting me on the walk. I need to do this more often. You riding with the girls today?"

"I don't know. Not sure my butt can take any more time in the saddle. I think I'll pass today."

Up ahead, the girls reached the back gate leading to the camp stable and opened it. Susan and Connie followed them in and were surprised to find the sheriff's car parked in the drive leading to the corral. Talking to the stable manager were a sheriff's deputy and an extremely agitated Brandon.

"Did you see Sarah?" Brandon shouted the moment he spotted Susan.

"Sarah?" Susan asked when she reached Brandon. She glanced from him to the deputy, who was now talking on his car's radio.

"Sarah's missing." Agitated, Brandon combed his fingers through his hair. Susan and her fellow hikers surrounded Brandon, wanting to know what was going on. The deputy stood about ten feet away at his car, still on the radio.

"What do you mean missing?" Susan asked. "Where's your sister?"

"She's back at the cabin talking to the ranger.

Sarah wanted to come see the horses today—wanted to see you," he told Susan. "She threw a major tantrum when I wouldn't bring her, so Kit put her in the bedroom for time out. When we went to check on her, she was gone."

"She ran away?" Lexi asked.

"We've looked everywhere in and around the cabin. We thought she might have tried to walk here on her own. Sarah never used to throw tantrums, but ever since her father was killed... Damn, why didn't I just bring her?"

Susan suspected he hadn't brought Sarah because he didn't want to see her, which made her feel somehow responsible.

"Her dad died?" Lexi asked.

"Yes," Susan answered. "In March."

"Poor kid. She must be terrified. We'll help you look," Lexi offered. A few minutes later, the sheriff's deputy got off the radio and began recruiting volunteers to help search for the missing child; by that time, Carol had joined the group and was anxious to help her friend.

The older girls at the camp—those most familiar with the trails surrounding the stables—teamed up in groups to systematically search the area with some making their way back to the cabin Brandon and his sister had rented.

Susan and Brandon didn't put up an argument when the deputy suggested they team up, heading in the direction of the more rugged trails between Brandon's cabin and the stables. Unlike Brandon, Susan was familiar with the area and still knew the local trails.

"When someone finds her, I'll have them ring the bell at the church camp, then everyone meet back here," the deputy told them. Brandon and Susan went to Carol's office to call Kit before starting on their search.

"I was hoping she would tell me Sarah was there… back at the cabin," Brandon told Susan when he got off the phone.

"Any chance she's hiding somewhere in the cabin? I assume you checked all the obvious places—under the beds, closets."

"Yes. That was our first thought. Like I said, Sarah has never run off like this before. But she really wanted to come see the horses again."

"How is your sister holding up?" Susan asked as she and Brandon left the office and headed toward the trail.

"I think it's driving her crazy that she can't get out there and search, but they want her to stay at the cabin in case Sarah shows up on her own. The ranger already has people down at the lake, but we don't think it would have been possible for her to get out there that quickly."

"Damn, the lake." Susan didn't like the idea of a little girl Sarah's age wandering around the water. "I hate to ask this, but are they considering the possibility of someone taking her? Picking her up in a car?"

"We immediately called the sheriff when we realized she was gone. Even if someone had taken her—God forbid—they wouldn't have been able to get off the mountain by that time. They're checking cars leaving the mountain at both exits. I guess it's standard protocol up here because of the two camps."

"That's true," Susan agreed. "Years ago, a little girl was abducted from the church camp. After that, if a young child is missing up on Shipley Mountain, they don't just search the area, they immediately close the two exit roads."

"That little girl… do you know what happened to her?" Brandon asked.

"It was a long time ago, Brandon. Back when I was a kid."

"Do you know if they found her?"

"Yes."

"Was she okay?"

"Sarah is going to be fine, Brandon. We will *find* her."

"Susan, what happened to that other little girl?"

Susan sighed before reluctantly answering. "They found her about 300 miles from here."

"Was she okay? Was she alive?"

"No. But, Brandon, you can't focus on the worst scenario. What happened back then... back then there were no road closures. And the fact it's cooler today is a plus because snakes don't like this cooler weather."

"Damn, snakes. I didn't even think about that," Brandon grumbled. "What other wildlife do we have to worry about?"

"We don't have to worry about anything. We simply need to find your niece," Susan insisted, sounding far more positive than she felt.

When they reached the trail, Brandon repeatedly called out Sarah's name. In the distance, they could hear other searchers calling out for Sarah.

"I wish the damn cell phones worked up here," Brandon said as they continued to hike up the trail. "How do we know if someone finds her?"

"They'll ring the church bell over the church camp," Susan explained.

"They will?"

"I guess you didn't hear the sheriff mention it. He told us he'd have them ring the bell when someone found her, and to meet back at the stables."

"Will we be able to hear the bell?"

"Oh, yeah. That sucker vibrates off the mountain. Haven't you heard it?"

"Now that you mention it, yes. I wondered what it was."

Susan led the way on the trail, and when they came to a fork, she hesitated for a moment. The plan was for her and Brandon to follow the north trail between Brandon's cabin and the stables. In that moment, Susan realized she didn't remember the trails as well as she had imagined. *It has been over six years*, she reminded herself. After considering the best course, she decided to go right instead of left.

"Nothing can happen to Sarah; I don't think Kit could handle it," Brandon told her.

"Your sister has certainly had more than her share of heartbreak this year."

"Kev—that was my brother-in-law—he was really a great guy. Good father, supportive husband. When my dad was sick, he was always there for both of us. He adored his daughter. I hate the thought he won't be able to see her grow up."

"She's lucky to have you, Brandon. I see how she looks at you."

"I know you thought she was mine."

"About that…"

"I'm sorry, Susan. I was too rough on you the other day. I am sorry. Sarah does look enough like me to be my daughter."

"She seems crazy about you."

Brandon called out Sarah's name before responding. "I'm pretty crazy about her, too. I remember when she was born—I was one of the first to see her, after Kev and Kit. They let me hold her; she was such a tiny thing. Damn, that kid just grabbed me by my heart and never let go."

"I think you'll be a good dad some day."

"I don't know if I want kids."

Susan paused a moment on the trail and looked at him. "Are you serious? The way you were talking the other day, I sort of got the feeling you were at that place.... like you wanted to find the right person and settle down with." *I guess I was assuming again,* she thought. *Assuming settling down meant starting a family.*

"That was before today—before Sarah took off. I don't know if I could handle this sort of emotional roller coaster. Kit says I'll love my own kids even more than Sarah. If that's true, then I'd never survive this kind of shit with my own kid. I don't think I'm tough enough."

"Do you ever pray?" Susan asked.

"Until today—not often. You?"

"I pray every day."

"I never was much for church," Brandon said.

"Praying doesn't have anything to do with going to church."

"So, you don't go to church?" Brandon asked.

"No... I go to church. I was just saying praying

and going to church don't necessarily go hand in hand."

"I've prayed a lot today—that's for damn sure."

Brandon called out Sarah's name again. Just as he did, thunder rumbled overhead.

"Damn," Brandon cursed. "Please don't tell me it's going to start raining."

As if some evil force had heard his concern, rain began falling. Instead of light sprinkles, it came down in a torrent, drenching them both in a matter of moments.

Fisting his hands, his feet planted firmly on the ground, Brandon looked up to the sky as rainwater drenched his face.

"No, God! You can't do this!" Brandon shouted at the top of his lungs.

In the next moment, a bell began to ring—the church camp bell. It continued to ring, the sound traveling through the mountain. *Sarah had been found.*

The thought that Sarah hadn't been found safe and whole did not enter Susan's mind. She knew from the depths of her soul that the little girl was safe —maybe even now with her mother.

"Is that what I think?" Brandon asked excitedly, listening to the sound of the ringing camp bell.

"Yes! Sarah has been found!"

Without thought, Susan leapt into Brandon's open arms—accepting his spontaneous celebratory hug. Laughing, he twirled her around, his feet slipping on the now muddy ground. When he finally released her, Susan was still laughing from relief. Stumbling a bit when he set her back on her feet, she misstepped and fell to the ground.

"Damn, I'm sorry," Brandon said, kneeling by her side.

Susan tried to stand up but discovered it was too painful to put weight on her right foot.

"Damn," Susan cried out, clutching her ankle, "I think I sprained my ankle." Rain continued to fall from the sky.

"Here, let me help you." Gently Brandon pulled Susan up as she balanced her weight on her left foot.

"Ouch," Susan said as she briefly touched her right toe to the ground. "Crap, I really screwed up my ankle. I don't think I can walk back."

"I'll carry you," Brandon offered. Susan looked up into Brandon's face and rolled her eyes.

"What?" he asked, noting her lack of confidence.

"You are a nice, big, strong guy, Brandon. But carry me back to the camp… in this weather? I don't think so. Maybe I can hop."

"Hop all the way?" Brandon removed his jacket and put it over Susan's head.

"Put your coat back on!" Susan scolded.

"You're getting soaked."

"And you aren't?" she asked.

When Brandon continued to hold the jacket over her head, she snatched it from him and shoved it against his chest, urging him to put it back on. The movement only made her stumble, putting unwanted pressure on her lame foot. She cried out in pain.

Brandon hastily slipped his jacket back on and took hold of Susan's left arm.

"If we could find some shelter until it stops raining... Maybe by that time, your ankle will feel better."

Susan wrapped her arm around Brandon's waist as he did the same to her. Leaning against him, she took little hops as he led her toward a shelter of the trees. Huddling under the limbs provided little protection from the rain. Lightning streaked across the sky followed by a clash of thunder.

"Not a good idea standing under these trees. The chapel," Susan suggested.

"What are you talking about?"

"Remember the little chapel the other day—the one you pulled me into? It's not far from here.

Together they made their way in the direction Susan suggested, moving with awkward hops. They continued on their way for about twenty minutes. Rain continued to come down, but now it was more in sprinkles than a steady downpour.

Moving through a small clearing, Brandon spied the chapel ahead. Tired of the incessant rain and the snail's pace, he swooped Susan up in his arms and started toward the chapel, his hiking boots sloshing in the muddy ground. Not prepared for the sudden motion, Susan let out a little cry of surprise and wrapped her arms around Brandon's neck, holding on tight.

"I'm too heavy for you," she whispered in his ear.

"I just want to get the hell out of this damn rain," he told her, determined to get to the chapel without having to put her down. The combination of pine needles and mud on the ground made for a slippery walkway. Several times, Brandon slid in the mud yet managed to keep his hold on Susan without falling with her to the ground.

Relieved at knowing Sarah had been found and finding humor in her current situation—especially considering Brandon's stubborn determination to carry her the rest of the way—made Susan giggle in spite of her throbbing ankle.

"What's so funny?" Brandon grumbled, his breathing now labored.

"If you think you're going to have a heart attack, please set me down first."

"I promise."

When Brandon reached the chapel, Susan expected him to set her down by the door. Instead, he managed to open the door while still holding her in his arms. After moving inside the small building, he set her down on the church pew.

"We made it!" Susan exclaimed, sitting on the oak pew. Clutching her injured foot, she slipped off the tennis shoe and sock. The ankle was slightly swollen.

"It doesn't look too bad." Brandon sat on the pew next to Susan. "Does it hurt?"

"Yes. Like a bitch."

CHAPTER SEVENTEEN

"I can't believe how warm it is in here," Brandon said as he attended to Susan's injury. Shirtless, he sat next to her on the church pew, her injured limb propped on his knee as he carefully wound the makeshift bandage, fashioned from his shirt's fabric, around her ankle.

"It's the way the sun hits the stained glass window, and it's a good thing, considering how soaked we are and that you're sitting there practically naked. Do you really know what you're doing?"

"I sacrifice my shirt for you, and you dare question my skill?" Brandon teased.

"I do feel bad about your shirt. It was a nice shirt. Ouch! That hurts; too tight."

"Sorry." Brandon loosened the bandage slightly and then continued on. "I couldn't stand much more of your moaning and wincing."

"I didn't moan. But I do cop to the wincing."

"There," Brandon said as he finished securing the bandage. "That should do it."

"It does feel better. Thanks." Susan didn't attempt to pull her foot from his knee, and Brandon didn't move from his place on the pew.

"Susan," Brandon asked in a serious tone. "I was just so damned relieved to hear that bell ring that I didn't stop to think. Do you think she's okay? We know they found her, but do you think she's alright?"

"I'm sure she's fine. The rain started about the same time the bell started ringing, so we know she wasn't wandering around in the rain. No chance of catching pneumonia. I can't recall the last time a wild animal—a dangerous wild animal—was seen this close to the camps or cabins."

"When was the last time you were up here?" By the tone of Brandon's question, it didn't sound as if he trusted her assessment.

"Okay, maybe it has been a number of years, and I suppose it is possible there've been wildlife sightings near the camps and cabins over the last few years, but we're talking nocturnal animals. If she was out overnight, then I'd be concerned. But in the middle of the afternoon? I seriously doubt it. The one thing that did concern me was the lake, but you said she wouldn't have had time to reach the water before the search party got there. I'm sure she's fine, and once this rain stops, you can go see for yourself."

"And leave you here alone?"

"I'll be fine. I'd try to convince you to go now to relieve your worry, but I don't think walking around in the rain and the lightning is a smart idea."

"I have to get you back to the camp, and there's no way to get my truck up here. I could try carrying you back."

"Carry me?" Susan laughed. "It about killed you when you carried me a hundred feet. No, I've already figured it out. Have Lexi and Andrea bring the horses up here. I can ride back to the camp."

"And how do you expect to get up on the horse?"

"Don't worry. You have the girls get the horses up here, and I'll get on one."

"I'm sorry I hurt your foot."

"You didn't hurt my foot. I tripped."

"Yes. After I dumped you on the ground."

Susan laughed. "You didn't dump me, *exactly*."

Brandon flashed Susan a grin but reserved comment. They sat for a few moments in silence, each lost in private thoughts while Susan's injured ankle rested on his knee.

"I'm sorry I acted like such a prick the other day —at the lake," Brandon said at last.

"I'm sorry I jumped to all the wrong conclusions about you," Susan countered in a quiet voice.

"Kit told me I was wrong. She said she understood why you'd jumped to the conclusions you did, especially considering the circumstances."

"Circumstances? Umm… just what did you tell your sister about me?"

"She knows we went out."

"Went out? Does she know we… you know…"

"Spent the night together?" Brandon asked with a smile.

"Yes."

"I told her."

"Oh… crap…" Susan closed her eyes for a minute. "What does she think of me, picking you up in a place like After Sundown?"

"I did *not* tell her about After Sundown. In fact, I'd prefer my sister wasn't told about that place—or what typically goes on there."

"I guess that makes me feel a little better… but just a little."

"I'm not in the habit of sharing details of my sex life with my sister. She just knew I was a little upset the other day, and I only told her we'd gone out— spent a night together—and that after, you assumed I was married, that Sarah was mine."

"I honestly didn't get your second note," Susan told him.

"I've sort of figured that out."

"But you didn't believe me at first, did you?"

"It wasn't that—*exactly.*"

"I just remembered something," Susan said shyly.

"What?"

"I don't even know your last name."

"I never told you my last name?" Brandon found that hard to believe.

"No, it never came up."

"Carpenter."

"Carpenter?" Susan frowned.

"My last name. Carpenter. My name is Brandon Carpenter."

"Carpenter?" Susan began to laugh. "You're in construction and your last name is *Carpenter*?"

"Someday, if I ever get around to getting my contractor's license I figure Carpenter Construction might be a good name for my company."

Susan smiled. "Are you considering getting your license?"

"I probably will someday. Can't do framing forever—tears up the body."

Your body looks pretty good to me, Susan thought, eyeing his exposed chest, the well-toned abs. He had little chest hair, and what he did have was blond and seemed to disappear against his tanned skin. Taking another look at his impressively formed biceps, she wondered if perhaps it might be easy for him to carry her back to the camp. *It was almost worth spraining my ankle to get you out of your shirt so I could admire this view.*

"What are you doing at the end of summer?" Brandon asked. "Going back to the school district?"

"No. I gave my notice at the end of the school year. Not sure what I want to do. I was hoping this time up here would give me a fresh perspective on the future. Maybe I'd come to some grand epiphany on what I should do with the rest of my life."

"And has it?"

"Not exactly. I still know I don't want to go back to the school district. But what do I want to do? Haven't a clue."

"I was curious why you moved. I thought you liked your new apartment."

"One reason—why pay rent on an apartment if I'm living up here for the summer?" *Another was that I didn't want you to know where I was.*

"Yeah, but you moved out before you came up here. Were you staying with friends?"

"My parents. I moved into my parents' house. One of the neighbors knew someone who wanted my unit, so it all worked out. I didn't lose any deposits or anything."

"Are you planning to go back to your parents' house after summer ends?"

"For a while, until I get settled. It is a little strange going back there, but it's not really a problem. No reason to get another apartment until I figure out what I'm going to do. And who knows? Maybe I'll pick up and move to another city—another state."

"Seriously? You'd leave your family and friends?"

Susan shrugged and said, "It's always a possibility. Not that I have any real desire to move from our area, but I'll consider all options."

"Your ex—is he still in the area? I think you mentioned he might get married. Did he?"

"Sam? No, he hasn't remarried. But it seems he and Loretta—that's his girlfriend—have an off and on thing of convenience going on. At least, that's what I gather from the grapevine."

"So you never see him anymore?"

"Only once—when he asked me to go back with him." Susan smiled at the memory.

"He asked you to go back with him?" Brandon asked incredulously.

"Hey, why wouldn't he want me back? I'm a great catch!" Susan said with a faux pout.

"That's not what I meant." Brandon gently patted her leg and flashed a smile. "It's just that you mentioned he was still with Loretta."

"Yes, but I said *off and on*. Oh, it wasn't that he suddenly realized he was madly in love with me. He'd just moved out of Loretta's—they were on the outs at the time—and he needed a place to stay. Plus, I had just deposited my share of the money from the house."

"You seem rather amused about it."

"I suppose I am, in a way. And no, I was not tempted to accept his offer of reconciliation."

"I didn't ask."

"No, but you were wondering, weren't you?"

Brandon shrugged and said, "I suppose the question crossed my mind. But it really is none of my business."

"Then why did you ask if I'd seen him?"

"Doesn't mean I'm not curious—even if I know it's none of my business." Brandon didn't say anything for a moment and then added, "Ah hell, I know it's none of my business—but why didn't you consider going back with him?"

"That's easy. I don't love him anymore. I'm starting to think I never did. No, let me rephrase that. I was in love with the man I thought he was. But the man he actually is, frankly, I don't even like that guy, much less love him. And, Brandon… that's one reason I jumped to the conclusions I did."

"I don't understand."

"After my divorce was finalized, my friends admitted they never really liked him. They pointed out that I… I tend to be too trusting. I decided to stop being a pushover, and instead of assuming the best… you get the idea."

"While I understand what you're saying, I don't think it's fair to judge a person by someone else's actions."

"I'm just talking about healthy skepticism."

"Perhaps. I can't speak for anyone else, but I'd rather I be judged on my own behavior, not on someone else's."

"I'm not saying I won't trust someone again, just

that trust needs to be earned. It's not something to hand over blindly. At least, not anymore," Susan said defensively. While she had begun to feel a little guilty about jumping to the conclusion that Brandon was married, she felt he was being unreasonable.

"I suppose it's all about the glass of water," Brandon said.

"What do you mean?"

"You know, the old *is the glass half empty or half full* thing. You choose to see it as half empty instead of half full."

"I don't see how that has anything to do with trying to be less naïve."

"Do you hear that?" Brandon asked, ignoring Susan's last comment.

"Hear what?" Susan frowned.

"It stopped raining." Gently, Brandon lifted Susan's ankle from his knee and set it on the pew as he stood up and walked to the door. Opening it, he stepped outside and looked up into the sky.

"How does it look?" Susan asked.

"It's pretty clear. I think the storm's over. Do you think you'll be okay here alone?"

"Certainly. It isn't that far to the camp; it shouldn't take you long."

CHAPTER EIGHTEEN

Pillowing the windbreaker under her head, Susan stretched out on the church pew. She didn't imagine she'd be stuck in the chapel for more than an hour, and quite possibly, the girls would show up within thirty minutes. The ground on Shipley Mountain tended to dry quickly after one of these storms, so she wasn't concerned about it being too muddy to take the horses out.

Her clothes had already dried, yet her hair was still a little damp. The ankle only hurt when she tried to put her foot on the floor or bumped it against the pew. She was tired and just wanted to rest before the girls arrived, yet she didn't want to fall asleep. While she felt relatively safe in the chapel, she didn't think it was wise to take a nap in an abandoned building when anyone might walk in. There was no way to lock the chapel door.

Looking up at the ceiling, she thought about her conversation with Brandon. It was obvious to her that he'd moved beyond whatever interest he once had in her. She supposed she should just be grateful that he no longer treated her with animosity.

The sound of someone turning the doorknob disrupted Susan's private thoughts. Instead of sitting up, she froze. It was too soon for the girls to arrive, and she couldn't imagine it was Brandon doubling back since he'd been gone for at least fifteen minutes. Silently, she lay on the pew and listened to the door open. Whoever it was would not be able to see her as the back of the pew faced the door.

"Little girl!" a woman's voiced whispered. "Come out from wherever you're hiding. We need to get you home before it starts raining again."

Little girl? Susan frowned. *Is someone still out looking for Sarah?*

Abruptly, Susan sat up and turned to face the intruder. An elderly woman stood in the doorway. Startled by Susan's sudden appearance, the woman jumped backwards, her eyes wide. Clad in navy blue sweat pants and matching sweatshirt, and wearing what appeared to be a strand of pearls around her neck, the woman had obviously been out in the rain because her gray hair was wet.

Susan thought she looked familiar but couldn't place her and wondered, *Who wears pearls with a jogging suit?*

"Who are you?" the woman asked, glancing around the small chapel. "What are you doing in here?"

"I hurt my ankle. I'm waiting for my friends to come get me. Are you looking for Sarah?" Susan sat up a little straighter and set both feet on the floor. She winced from the sudden pain when her right foot pressed against the hardwood floor. Lifting the foot slightly to alleviate the pain, she waited for the woman's answer.

"Sarah? Who's Sarah?" The woman frowned.

"The little girl who was missing. I assume you were in one of the search parties?"

"Search parties? I don't know what you're talking about. This Sarah… she's missing?"

"She was. Didn't you hear the camp bell ringing?"

"Yes, I heard it. But what does it have to do with the missing child?"

"They had search parties out looking for her. We were all told that when she was found, they'd ring the bell."

"Oh," the woman glanced around the room. "Sorry I disturbed you."

"Wait," Susan called out as the woman turned to leave.

"What?" Standing at the doorway, the woman glanced back to Susan.

"Who were you looking for?" Susan asked.

"Excuse me?" The woman frowned.

"When you came in here, you said, *Little girl come out from wherever you're hiding.*"

"Oh, that." The woman smiled. "My granddaughter. We were playing a game. I thought she was in here, but obviously, she isn't."

"You were playing a game in the rain?" Susan frowned.

"It isn't raining right now."

"No, but it was."

"I'm not sure I get your point."

"You look familiar," Susan said.

"You don't," the woman countered.

"It's been a few years since I was up here. I just wondered if we met before."

"Do you have a cabin up here?" the woman asked.

"No, but I used to spend summers here."

"I suppose it's possible we've met before. I've been spending my summers up here for over twenty years."

"Your granddaughter spends the summers with you?" Susan asked.

"My granddaughter?" The woman frowned.

"Yes, the one you were looking for."

"I need to get going. I have dinner to make." The woman turned abruptly and left the chapel.

"That was odd," Susan said aloud to the empty room. Less than thirty minutes later, Lexi and Andrea arrived on horseback, and they weren't alone. Brandon was with them.

"I didn't expect to see you," Susan said after she hopped to the door on her good foot and looked outside. There were four horses and three riders. Holding onto the door jam to maintain balance, she watched as Brandon dismounted from his horse.

"I don't think he trusted us to get you up on the saddle," Lexi said with a laugh. "You feel okay, Susan?"

"Actually, it's feeling a lot better. Doesn't hurt as much. I can even put a little pressure on it."

"Don't push it," Brandon said. He handed his reins to Lexi while Andrea held the reins to the horse Susan would be riding.

"Yes, sir," Susan chuckled. "How is Sarah?"

"She's fine—back at the cabin with Kit. I haven't seen her yet, but I gave Kit a call from Carol's office."

Andrea jumped off her mount and led Susan's horse to her, holding the mare in placed while Brandon awkwardly helped Susan onto the saddle. Once she was seated, he and Andrea remounted, and the four started on their way down the trail.

"Carol called the doctor," Lexi told her. "She wants you to go to the village and have your ankle looked at when we get back."

"I told her I'd drive you down. It's the least I can do for Carol considering how helpful the camp was in finding Sarah."

Susan was a little disappointed that he added the reason for offering her a ride. It would have been nice if he simply wanted to spend more time with her.

"I don't know if I need to see a doctor."

"I don't think that's an option Carol will consider," Brandon said.

"I suppose you're right. So, where did they find your niece?" Susan asked.

"I'm not sure; I just know she's with her mom. I'll find out more when I get back to the cabin."

"I had a strange visitor when I was waiting for you guys," Susan said, speaking loudly so they could all hear.

"Visitor? What do you mean?" Brandon asked.

"This older woman stopped by looking for her granddaughter."

"Older woman?" Andrea asked.

"I don't know how old she was, but she looked older than my grandmother. About my height, plump, wearing a blue jogging suit. Short, gray hair. She didn't give her name, but I know I've seen her before."

"Sounds a little like the lady who has a cabin over on Pine Street," Lexi said.

"Pine Street? Isn't that the next street over from where we're staying?" Brandon asked.

"Yes," Lexi answered. "But now that I think of it, she couldn't have a granddaughter. She doesn't have any kids."

"Maybe she has grown kids with children?" Susan suggested.

"No, I remember she had a little girl who died years ago. Never had any other children. It's just her and her husband; they come up here every summer. But if you say she was with her granddaughter, then it was probably someone else. I just thought of her because I've seen her around a few times this summer, and she's always wearing the same old blue jogging suit."

"I didn't say she was with her granddaughter. She was *looking* for her."

"I don't understand." Lexi frowned.

"She came into the chapel and said, *little girl come out from your hiding place,* or something like that. And then told her they needed to get back to the cabin. At first, I thought she was from the search party and looking for Sarah. But when I asked, she didn't seem to know anything about Sarah being missing. It was just weird."

"Maybe it is her," Lexi suggested. "The woman I'm thinking of is a little odd. Seems kind of out of it. Wouldn't surprise me if she has an imaginary granddaughter."

"You say she lives with her husband?" Brandon asked.

"Yes. Why?" Lexi asked.

"Trail's Chapel seems a strange place for her to be wandering alone, away from the cabins. When we get back, someone might want to check with her husband and see if she's okay. That's *assuming* she's the same woman Susan saw. I'd hate to think of her wandering alone in the forest."

"You think she might be suffering from dementia or something?" Susan asked.

"Lexi just mentioned she seemed out of it and acted odd. An elderly woman hiking alone so far from the cabins makes me wonder if she's okay."

"I hadn't thought about that," Susan said, feeling a bit guilty for not being more concerned at the time. However, the woman appeared to be capable and in possession of her faculties. Then she remembered the pearls. *Okay, now that was peculiar. Who wears pearls with sweats?*

"Lexi, any chance does the woman you mentioned wear pearls with her jogging suit?" Susan asked.

"Pearls?" Andrea laughed at the thought.

"That's right," Lexi said after a moment. "I always thought pearls and sweats made a strange outfit. But yeah, she wears pearls."

When they reached the stables, Carol was waiting for them.

"How are you feeling?" Carol asked as she took the reins so Brandon could help Susan from the horse.

"I feel much better. It is a little tender still, but I don't think I need to see a doctor."

"I'd rather we make sure it isn't something serious. I insist," Carol told her.

"Susan mentioned she ran into an elderly woman up at the chapel," Brandon told Carol. "I guess she lives over on Pine Street. Odd lady, normally wears blue sweats and pearls."

"You mean Harriet Summers," Carol said.

"You know her?" Susan asked.

"Sure. Harriet and Ed Summers have had a cabin up here for as long as I can remember. She is kind of an odd duck."

"We were wondering if maybe we should check in with her husband, make sure she's okay, that she got home alright," Brandon said. "Seemed like an odd place for her to be hiking alone."

"Actually, it's not," Carol said. "Harriet has been hiking these trails for years, normally alone. Her husband used to hike with her, but he's been confined to a wheel chair for some time now."

"Do you know if she has a granddaughter?" Susan asked.

"Granddaughter? They don't have any children. Why?" Carol asked.

"When I was waiting alone in the chapel, she came in and said something like *little girl are you in here*. At first, I assumed she was looking for Sarah, but she told me she didn't know about Sarah and said she was looking for her granddaughter."

"Hmm, that is odd." Carol frowned.

"Perhaps she really was looking for Sarah," Susan suggested. "Maybe she felt silly looking after I mentioned she had already been found. She admitted hearing the bell yet didn't seem to understand what it meant."

"Now, that's entirely possible," Carol agreed.

CHAPTER NINETEEN

"Thanks for driving me to the village. If it had been my left ankle, I think I could have driven myself." Susan sat in the passenger side of Brandon's truck as they drove down the mountain road.

"No problem. I'm happy to do it. And I want to thank you again for helping us look for Sarah."

"I'm just relieved they found her safe and sound."

"Yeah, you and me both. I can't even imagine how Kit would have handled losing Sarah. Or even worse—if we never found her. I don't know how parents cope with that kind of loss."

"Being a parent makes you damn vulnerable, that's for sure."

"So can being an uncle," Brandon grumbled.

"Were you serious when you said you didn't think you wanted kids someday?"

"I don't know… probably not."

"You mean you don't want them?"

"No," Brandon chuckled. "I meant I probably wasn't serious. Sarah just scared the crap out of me."

"She's okay, so that's all that really matters."

"Do you want kids someday?" Brandon asked.

"I've always wanted to have children. Funny thing, last year, Sam and I talked about starting a family. Of course, I didn't know he had a lover at the time."

"You mean, when you were talking about starting a family, he was screwing around?"

"Yep."

"What an ass," Brandon grumbled.

They were quiet for a few moments when Susan asked, "Did you guys just bring your truck up here?"

"No, Kit drove her Suburban up. Why?

"Oh, I don't know. Just wondered if the three of you traveled up here in this."

"Kit's not thrilled when Sarah drives in the truck with me."

"She doesn't like your driving? Do I need to be worried?" Susan teased

"No, it's not that." Brandon grinned. "It's safer to put car seats in the back seat of a car. Although, there've been a few times these last few months we had no choice."

Susan remembered he had been driving his truck when she'd first seen him with Sarah.

"So why didn't you just drive up with her in the Suburban? Why two cars?"

"I needed my truck for work."

"I don't understand." Susan frowned.

"I wanted to get Kit and Sarah away for the summer—out of the city, away from all the crap they've been dealing with. Carol helped find us a cabin to rent, and she hooked me up with some work for the summer. This past week has been my vacation. But next week, I go back to work, starting with rebuilding a porch on a cabin a couple of blocks from ours. And then there is a roof… You get the idea."

"A work vacation."

"Sort of."

"So, how does Carol know Kit? Someone said something about a restaurant expo?"

"A number of years ago, Carol attended a restaurant expo—for the camp. You know, checking out equipment and new ideas for the mess hall. Kit went to the expo that year and met Carol. The two hit if off, and they've been friends ever since. A couple of summers ago Kit and Kev rented a cabin up here."

"That's right; you mentioned Kit was in the restaurant business."

"She hasn't been working much since Sarah's birth—wanted to be a full time mom and stay at home. I'm afraid that's not an option now that Kevin has been killed."

"Did he have life insurance?" Susan immediately regretted the question. *It is none of my business.*

"Yes, but it'll only provide a cushion—it won't support them indefinitely."

"They're lucky to have you."

"I am lucky to have them," Brandon insisted.

They rode in silence for the next five minutes as Brandon steered the truck down the winding mountain road. Turning slightly in the passenger seat, Susan leaned against the truck door and watched Brandon, studying his profile. He glanced briefly in her direction, and she gave him a smile.

"Susan, I was wondering..." Brandon didn't finish his sentence.

"What?" Susan asked a few moments later. He glanced back at her, and then put his eyes back on the mountain road.

"I was wondering if we could try again."

"Try again?" Susan's heartbeat accelerated.

"Maybe we could go out sometime. I don't know how it works for you at the camp, if you can get any time off. But I'll be up here all summer. Maybe we could go down to the village sometime for dinner or maybe go fishing next weekend... if you can get away and if... if you're interested."

Susan couldn't help but smile.

"I think I would like that, Brandon."

Brandon glanced at Susan and grinned.

WHEN BRANDON ARRIVED BACK AT HIS CABIN, HE found his sister and niece in the kitchen. Kit stood at the sink drying dishes while Sarah sat at the table eating a bowl of macaroni and cheese. Brandon went immediately to his niece and gave her a hug and kiss.

Sarah ignored her uncle's attentions, nudging him away as she took another bite of food. Brandon glanced up at his sister and gave her a questioning frown. Kit tossed the dishtowel she had been using down on the counter and nodded to Brandon to follow her into the other room.

"She didn't seem thrilled to see me," Brandon said when he and Kit were in the living room.

"She's been like that ever since she got home. How is Susan's ankle?"

"The doctor said it was fine. He just wanted her to stay off it for the rest of the day. So tell me, who found Sarah—and where was she?"

"No one found her, Brandon; she just came home. I was sitting on the front porch hoping to hear that church bell ring when she came running up the drive and into my arms. I asked her where she'd been, and she just said she'd gone to look for the horses and got lost. I asked her where she'd been all that time, and she said nowhere."

"Nowhere?"

"I took that to mean she was trying to find the

stables—or the cabin—so in her mind she wasn't anywhere she could describe."

"But what is with the attitude?"

"That's probably my fault. After the initial relief having her home safe, I sort of flipped out. I started lecturing her—too much for a four-year-old. She started crying, I started crying—it was awful. I finally settled down and got her to stop crying. She just wanted to go play with her dolls, which she has been doing most of the afternoon since she came home."

"But still has the attitude," Brandon grumbled.

"She was scared Brandon, and I imagine she's tired. It's been a long day for her… for all of us. When she's finished eating, I'm giving her a bath and putting her to bed."

Thirty minutes later, Brandon was relaxing in front of the television in the living room while Kit gave Sarah a bath.

"Brandon!" Kit shouted from the bathroom. "Get in here!

Jumping up from the couch, Brandon raced to his sister. He found Kit sitting on the floor of the bathroom next to the tub, shampooing Sarah's long blonde hair while Sarah played with her bath toys. The little girl seemed to pay no notice to the sudden appearance of her uncle or her mother's recent shout.

"What's wrong?" Brandon asked from the doorway.

"Look at this," Kit said in a quiet voice as she held

a soapy lock of her daughter's hair. Sarah continued to play with her toys, scooping up water with a plastic toy shovel and then dumping it into a small red bucket.

Brandon walked into the bathroom and went to one knee beside Kit. He looked at what she held in her hand. A lock of hair had been cut from the back of Sarah's head. Instead of reaching to the center of her back, as did most of the hair, this piece was about three inches long.

"Her hair's been cut," Kit said. "It wasn't like this yesterday. Yesterday, I French-braided it. I would have noticed this. And today, before I sent her to time out, I unbraided her hair. It had to have been cut after that. I never noticed the missing hair. She has so much, and it was so curly from the braid."

"Sarah," Brandon said.

She looked up from the soapy water. "Yes, Uncle Brandon?"

"Did you play with a scissors today?"

"Mommy left my scissors at home."

"But did you happen to find a scissors somewhere?"

"I don't remember."

"Did you cut your hair, Sarah?" Brandon asked.

"I don't want short hair. I don't want to be a boy. Cinderella has long hair."

"Sarah," Kit said patiently, "a piece of your hair has been cut back here. I need to know how that happened. Did you find a scissors and try cutting your hair?"

"No, Mommy. Cinderella has long hair. I don't want to cut my hair."

"Okay, honey, but do you have any idea how your hair got cut?"

Sarah didn't answer. Instead, she started to play with her bath toys again.

"Sarah, I asked you a question. Do you know how your hair got cut?" Kit repeated.

"I don't want to talk about this," Sarah said stubbornly.

"Sarah, your mommy isn't going to be mad at you… even if you cut it yourself. We just need to know. I promise, Mommy will not be mad," Brandon said.

"I didn't cut my hair."

"But you know how it got cut, don't you?" Brandon coaxed.

"The bath's cold, Mommy." Sarah shivered. Pulling her knees to her chest, she wrapped her arms around her wet little body.

"I'll wait in the living room," Brandon said, leaving the bathroom so Kit could rinse off Sarah and get her from the tub.

When Sarah finally came out of the bathroom, she was wearing flannel pajamas. Her hair, which had been towel-dried, was still damp.

"Brandon, Sarah wanted to know if you would tell her a story before she goes to bed."

"Sure, I'd love to." He glanced up at his sister and gave her an inquisitive look. She understood what he was asking and shook her head no. Sarah had not revealed how her hair had managed to get cut.

Once in the bedroom Sarah was using, Kit pulled down the bed's sheet and comforter. Sarah scampered onto the mattress and wiggled against the pile of pillows as her mother covered her. Lifting up her arms, Sarah wrapped them around Kit's neck and gave her a hug.

"I love you, Mommy."

"I love you too, Sarah."

"I'm sorry, Mommy. I shouldn't have gone to see the horses."

"I know, honey. Mommy was very worried. Please promise to never do something like that again."

"I promise, Mommy."

Kit gave her daughter a tight hug, and then kissed her on the forehead before leaving the room.

Brandon made himself comfortable on the bed next to Sarah. Book in hand, he lay atop the comforter and leaned against the headboard.

"I have your favorite story here," Brandon said as he opened the small book. "*Once upon a time, there was a young girl who was sweet, kind and pretty.*" Brandon read the first line from *Cinderella*, and then kissed Sarah's forehead. "Kind of like you," he added.

"The lady cut my hair," Sarah blurted out.

"What did you say?" Brandon frowned.

"The lady cut my hair."

"What lady?"

"I don't know."

"What do you mean you don't know? What lady cut your hair?"

"I don't want Mommy to be mad at me again."

"Sarah, your mommy isn't going to be mad at you. But she needs to know what lady cut your hair so she can protect you."

"She said she would call Mommy, and when we went inside, she gave me a cookie. But then she started to cut my hair. I don't want to be a boy. Mommy is going to be mad at me for taking a cookie from a stranger."

CHAPTER TWENTY

*B*randon stood at the end of the driveway, his fingertips tucked casually into the back pockets of his denims as he watched the sheriff's car pull away. Disgusted with the officer's cavalier attitude, Brandon wanted to kick something. Just before he succumbed to the urge, he noticed a car pull into his neighbor's driveway. Immediately, he recognized its driver—*Susan*. Smiling to himself, Brandon silently watched as she parked and got out of the vehicle, then turned in his direction and smiled.

Damn, she looks good, Brandon thought. She wore denim shorts and a camp T-shirt, and the way her long dark hair was pulled up into a high ponytail made her look more like one of the girls at the camp rather than an adult counselor. A red purse hung casually over her right shoulder. It was a stark contrast from the first time he had met her. Then she had reminded him of a sleek young executive who looked as if she had just stepped out of the boardroom still wearing her fitted business suit and high heels. He had the same reaction to both versions—he wanted to strip off her clothes.

He was no longer annoyed with her for jumping to the wrong conclusions. Spending time with Susan made it impossible for him to harbor a grudge. She was different from other women he'd dated—definitely not high maintenance. It wasn't that she didn't always look good; it was more that she didn't seem to try to achieve a certain look. He imagined she'd taken maybe five minutes to get ready that morning, yet he couldn't imagine the results being more appealing had she spent the entire morning grooming and primping.

"Good morning," Susan greeted, walking down the driveway in his direction. Brandon grinned and started walking toward her.

"Why aren't you at work? Playing hooky?" he asked.

"Something like that. The girls went on an all-day trail ride, and Carol told me not to go."

"How's your ankle?" Brandon glanced down at her foot. She didn't appear to have a problem walking.

"It's a little sore but nothing major. How's Sarah

this morning? I noticed the sheriff's car leaving. Any problem?"

"Have Brandon come join us for coffee!" Connie, who had just opened her front door, called down from her front porch.

"Want to come over for coffee?" Susan asked before Brandon could answer her first set of questions.

"Sure, coffee sounds good."

Together Brandon and Susan headed to the Lewis cabin.

"So, how's Sarah doing this morning?"

"I guess she's okay," Brandon said with a shrug.

"You guess?" Susan frowned.

"I'll explain it over coffee," Brandon said.

Twenty minutes later, Brandon sat with Connie and Susan on the front porch of the cabin, coffee cup in hand. He'd just told about Sarah's cut hair and the officer's reaction.

"He didn't think it was worth looking into?" Connie asked.

"He seemed to believe Sarah had somehow cut her own hair and created an imaginary woman to take the blame. Unfortunately, Sarah wasn't willing— or able—to give us more information on this woman."

"Do you seriously think someone cut her hair? And why?" Susan asked.

"The only thing I can think of is… abduction. And

that scares the hell out of me." Brandon took a sip of his coffee. "Which is why the officer's reaction pisses me off."

"Abduction?" Connie asked.

"I think I know what you mean," Susan said. "You often hear how kidnappers cut a child's hair to change their appearance. You hear of that happening in bathrooms at amusement parks."

"That's a creepy thought!" Connie shuddered. "But why didn't she finish cutting her hair?"

"Like I said, by the time Sarah told us about this woman she was already in bed. We went ahead and called the sheriff last night but told them they wouldn't be able to talk to Sarah until this morning. She was sleeping by then. And this morning, before they arrived, I had another talk with Sarah. As best as I can determine, something interrupted the woman, and she left Sarah alone for a moment. Sarah was frightened and didn't want her hair cut, so she managed to slip out the woman's back door. Unfortunately, she can't seem to remember anything about where this woman lived or what she looked like. And when the sheriff was here, she basically said nothing."

"She didn't tell the officer about the woman cutting her hair?" Susan asked.

"Not really. I think she was afraid. The best we could do was get her to answer yes and no questions, and when the officer started questioning her in detail about this woman, he basically got Sarah to say she had made it up."

"But you don't think that's true?" Connie asked.

"No, I don't. Call it a gut feeling."

"What's your sister think?" Susan asked

"She's uncomfortable about the whole thing and determined to keep Sarah close at hand. One thing I'm fairly certain of, I don't think Sarah will be running away again. She was genuinely frightened."

"I suppose that's a good thing—maybe the one good thing out of all this. What are you going to do now?" Susan asked.

"The deputy just left, so I haven't had a chance to talk to Kit about it."

"I'm sorry he wasn't more helpful," Susan said.

"No kidding," Connie agreed.

"Me, too. So, what are you ladies up to today? Susan, when do you have to get back to the camp?" Brandon asked.

"When Connie found out I was on my own today, she invited me over to have coffee and see her newest painting," Susan explained.

"You paint?" Brandon asked.

"Connie is a very talented artist," Susan told him. "She has a gallery showing coming up."

"I'm impressed." Brandon smiled.

"Thank you." Connie blushed. "That's one reason I decided to spend the summer up here with Ella.

Gives me a quiet place to paint while Ella works at the camp."

"Where are your parents? I thought they were up here?" Susan asked.

"They were here last weekend, but they had to go home and back to work. They'll probably be up in a couple of weeks."

"If it wasn't for this thing with Sarah, I'd be looking forward to spending the rest of the summer here. But frankly, I'm a little uneasy now," Brandon said.

"I've always thought of this as such a safe place," Connie said.

"Susan mentioned something about a child once being kidnapped from one of the camps years ago," Brandon said.

"Oh, the Collins girl. That was a long time ago. I was in grade school back then. Nothing like that's ever happened again up here," Connie said. "And she wasn't taken from one of the camps. She was too young to attend camp. From what I remember, her older sister was at church camp, and she was staying with an aunt and uncle who had a cabin up here. I remember it was pretty awful."

"Susan said they found her about 300 miles away."

"They found her body; someone had left it outside a church." Connie said. "From what I was told, she hadn't been sexually abused. I remember hearing my parents discuss the case. The authorities didn't feel the kidnapper intended to kill her. The only injuries on her body seemed to have come from a fall that probably killed her."

"Did they catch the kidnapper?" Brandon asked.

"No. I remember they looked into the parents for a while, but no," Connie explained. "You don't think this has anything to do with Sarah's experience yesterday, do you?"

"No, not really. But I have to admit, hearing her talk about some woman cutting her hair makes me wonder if there's more to this than a little girl just wandering away on her own."

"Do you think it would be alright if I stop and see Sarah?" Susan asked. "I'm not planning to bug Connie much longer."

"Hey, you aren't bugging me." Connie laughed.

"No, but I only stopped over for a quick cup of coffee and to see your current painting before heading back to the camp. I don't want to keep you from your work."

"Sorry, that's my fault, keeping you both so long," Brandon said.

"Don't be silly, you two. This has been an interesting conversation," Connie insisted.

"Thanks, but I won't keep you any longer. Susan, before you leave, stop by my cabin and say hello to Sarah."

As it turned out, Brandon and Susan left Connie's

cabin together twenty minutes later, after they had both admired Connie's painting. Brandon resisted the urge to take Susan's hand in his as they made their way up the walk to his cabin.

"Are you okay driving with that ankle?" Brandon asked as they neared his cabin's front door.

"Why, do I look incapable?"

"No, you look rather nice."

"Are you making fun of me?" she asked with a laugh. Pausing a moment, she glanced down her body to her ankle, suddenly wishing she'd taken more care in getting ready that morning.

"No, I'm damn serious," Brandon insisted. Susan blushed at his compliment. Instead of going directly into the cabin, they stood for a moment on its front porch facing each other.

"You know what I keep wanting to call you?" Brandon asked in a low voice as he reached out with one hand and lightly brushed his fingertips down the side of her face.

"What?" Susan asked—her throat dry and heart pounding.

"*Brown-Eyed Beauty*. I thought that the first time I saw you," Brandon said with a grin.

Blushing again, Susan glanced down. "Are you trying to seduce me, Brandon Carpenter?" she asked in a quiet voice.

"I figure it's only fair. You seduced me the first time; now it's my turn."

Her gaze flashed up to meet his intent stare and her eyes widened as she noted the serious expression on Brandon's face. Before she could consider what was happening, he leaned closer and brushed his lips over hers. She closed her eyes briefly, startled at the electric sensation from such a fleeting intimacy. Brandon didn't apologize for—or explain—the kiss but led her into his cabin a moment later.

"Hello, Sarah," Susan greeted Brandon's niece when they walked into the kitchen. By the looks of the dishes on the table, it was obvious Kit and Sarah had just finished eating breakfast. While Sarah was dressed for the day, Kit wore a robe over what appeared to be pajamas.

"Hi, Susan!" Sarah said excitedly. "Did you ride a horse over?"

"No, I'm afraid I didn't." Susan smiled.

"Hello, Susan," Kit greeted with a smile. "Thanks for helping look for Sarah yesterday. Is your ankle feeling better?"

"I'm just relieved she's home. As for my ankle, it's almost as good as new."

"If you two will excuse me, I'm going to go get dressed. Brandon, make sure your niece doesn't escape while I'm gone."

"I don't think she was entirely joking," Susan said after Kit left the room.

"I have to agree with you," Brandon said as he sat at the table with his niece after pulling out a chair for Susan. She sat down with Brandon and Sarah.

"I understand you had quite the adventure yesterday," Susan told Sarah.

"I wanted to come see you and the horses, but I got lost."

"Yes, I heard that. We were sure worried about you but very happy to have you home with your mom and Uncle Brandon."

"A lady cut my hair." Sarah's announcement surprised Brandon, considering she'd practically refused to discuss it with the officer.

"Was this an old lady, like a grandma, or a young lady, like your mom?" Susan asked immediately.

"She was like a grandma," Sarah said. "But she had a princess necklace."

"A princess necklace?" Susan glanced at Brandon.

"Like Cinderella… the one the mean stepsister broke."

"Pearls… If I remember correctly, Cinderella was getting ready to go to the ball, and the stepsister ripped off the pearls she was wearing," Susan said thoughtfully.

"Yes! But hers were white," Sarah explained.

"Whose were white?" Susan asked.

"The lady. The lady who cut my hair. Her princess necklace was white."

Momentarily speechless, Susan looked up into Brandon's face. He was staring at her, and by his expression, he was obviously thinking the same thing as she was… *The woman wore pearls.*

"Do you remember what kind of clothes the woman was wearing? Maybe the color of her clothes?"

Sarah thought a moment and then said, "She was wearing blue pajamas."

"Why didn't you say anything to your sister about the pearls?" Susan asked Brandon as the two sat alone on the back porch of the rental cabin. Kit had just left ten minutes earlier with Sarah, driving over to the camp to visit with Carol.

"I didn't want to freak her out right now. At least not until I figure out what we should do about it."

"Are you going to call the sheriff's office again?"

"I'm not sure. What do I tell them? The woman wore a princess necklace? They'll just say this is more of Sarah's make believe."

"Didn't Carol say she knew the woman with the pearls? Assuming it is the same woman. But I can't believe there is more than one woman running around Shipley Mountain wearing blue sweat pants and pearls. Of course, Sarah didn't say her woman was wearing sweat pants, *exactly.*"

"I wonder if your friend Connie knows this woman. After all, she just lives on the next street over."

"Maybe we should go talk to Connie about her. See what she knows," Brandon suggested.

"You must mean Harriet Summers," Connie said as she used a stained rag to clean paint from her brush. Susan and Brandon had found Connie on the back porch of her cabin working at her easel.

"That's right. That's the name Carol said," Susan confirmed.

"They've had their cabin up here longer than us. She's never been particularly friendly that I can recall. But I remember her husband, Ed, was always a friendly guy, at least until the accident."

"Carol mentioned he was in a wheel chair. Was that from the accident you're talking about?" Susan asked.

"Yeah. From what I understand, he had a bad fall —broke his spinal cord I think. Before the accident, I remember him being very friendly. He has a work-shop in the back of their cabin, and when they'd come up for weekends, he'd make birdhouses for all the neighbors. He gave me one once; I used it as a dollhouse. There were a few times he helped Dad work on the cabin. But after the accident, he changed.

I remember Dad telling us how he stopped over to see him a few times after the accident, but Ed pretty much brushed him off. It was like that with all the neighbors. Now when they come up, he stays inside the cabin. You rarely see him on the porch in his chair."

"That's sad. How long has he been in a wheelchair?" Susan asked.

"Let's see…" Connie considered the question for a moment. "I remember it was the summer after the Collins girl disappeared. Shipley Mountain pretty much closes down for the winter—lake freezes over, and we don't have any ski lifts to attract winter visitors. Our family usually makes it up for Thanksgiving and sometimes Christmas. I don't remember seeing the Summerses that winter—the winter after the Collins child disappeared. But the next summer, when the Summerses returned to their cabin, he was in a wheelchair."

"I understand their only child died when she was just a little girl," Susan said.

"Why all the questions over the Summerses?" Carol asked.

"According to Sarah, the woman who cut her hair was wearing a pearl necklace," Brandon explained.

"Ekkk," Carol squeaked. "That gave me chills!"

"Why?" Susan frowned.

"Ed was always a nice guy, at least until the accident. But Harriet… there was always something a little creepy about her. When Ella and I would walk by her cabin, she would always stare at us and ask if we wanted to come in for cookies. But something about her sort of made me uneasy. I once mentioned it to my mom, who promptly reminded me that Harriet had had a rough life, first losing their only child and then having to care for an invalid husband. While I understood what Mom was saying, I still couldn't shake my feeling toward Harriet. And the idea of her cutting Sarah's hair doesn't really shock me."

"Then maybe you should call the sheriff again!" Susan told Brandon.

"I don't think so." Connie shook her head.

"Why not?" Susan asked.

"Do you remember the name of the officer that showed up this morning?" Connie asked.

"Anderson, I believe. Joe or James Anderson," Brandon said.

"That would be James Anderson. Harriet's baby brother. I don't think he will be of much help."

"Seriously? Her brother is the sheriff?"

"Not *the* sheriff, but yeah, he's one of the deputies," Connie told her. "He's not a bad guy, but I think it's a fairly close family, and I don't imagine he'd appreciate you coming to him with a story about his sister cutting Sarah's hair, especially if you don't have any proof."

"Do you know what happened to their daughter?" Susan asked.

"She drowned."

"Up here?" Brandon asked.

"No, in the ocean. This was before they had a cabin up here," Connie said.

———

"WHAT ARE YOU GOING TO DO NOW?" SUSAN ASKED Brandon after they left the Lewis cabin.

"Are you up to taking a little drive with me?" Brandon asked.

"Where to?"

"Pine Street."

"Sure… but what are you going to do?" Susan asked nervously.

"I have absolutely no idea." Brandon took Susan's hand in his and led her to his truck.

"I guess we should have asked Connie which house was the Summerses'," Susan said when they reached Pine Street. Brandon drove slowly down the quiet road, and she noted that most of the cabins on the narrow street seemed to be closed up.

"I don't know about that," Brandon said, bringing the truck to a stop in front of a blue cabin with a gambrel roof. Its front window was open, and from the street, Brandon could clearly see one of its occupants—a man sitting in a wheel chair.

"Now what?" Susan asked with a whisper, seeing what Brandon was looking at.

"I'd sort of like to see the inside of the house. Maybe there's something in there that Sarah might remember. She told you about the pearls today. Maybe she'll start remembering other things, like what was in the woman's kitchen. If her memories match up to something tangible, I could call the sheriff's office again."

"What about what Connie said? That deputy is Harriett's brother."

"I'll just make sure I talk to someone else."

"I have an idea," Susan suggested. "Remember, I met her yesterday up at the chapel. Let's just go up and knock on the door. I'll say I wanted to make sure Harriet got home okay—that Carol told me who she was and I was worried about her."

"Not sure if that will get us in the door, especially if she answers it."

"Well…" Susan considered her options for a moment. "I'll ask to use their bathroom. Would they really turn me down after I so thoughtfully stopped by to check on her?"

"Ah, what the hell… It's worth a shot," Brandon said. "Just remember, if this Harriet did cut Sarah's hair, then she could be dangerous… and so could her husband."

"The man is in a wheel chair, and I think I could take that woman. But if I see any firearms or dangerously sharp objects, I promise to make a hasty exit."

"Deal," Brandon said.

Once they reached the front door, Susan took a deep breath and gave a little nod to Brandon, who knocked loudly on the front of the cabin. After a second knock, the door opened. Susan and Brandon looked down into the unsmiling face of Ed Summers, who sat in a wheelchair.

"Yes, can I help you with something?" Ed asked.

"Hello," Susan said brightly. "I was wondering if Harriet was home."

"Who are you?" Ed narrowed his eyes.

"My name's Susan Thomas and this is my friend Brandon. I'm one of the counselors over at Camp Shipley. I met Harriet yesterday and wanted to make sure she got home okay."

"You met her where?" Ed asked.

"Up at Trail's Chapel after yesterday's storm."

"She isn't here right now." It was obvious Ed was anxious to shut the door.

"But she did get home okay yesterday? I was worried about her. It took me a while to figure out where she lived, or I would have been here earlier," Susan lied.

"Well... that is thoughtful of you. But Harriet got home fine. She just isn't here right now."

"Do you know when she might be back?"

"She drove down to the village to do some

grocery shopping and run some errands. I don't expect her back for a couple hours."

"Please tell her I stopped by… Oh, I have a big favor to ask you…" Susan glanced down as if embarrassed.

"Yes?"

"Is there any possible way I could use your bathroom? This is so embarrassing…"

"Sure." Ed rolled his wheelchair backwards, making room for Susan and Brandon to enter.

"Thank you so much!" Susan walked into the cabin and glanced around. "What a nice cabin." In truth, she thought it looked a little depressing. There was nothing cozy and comforting about the front room.

"Bathroom's through the kitchen." Ed pointed to a doorway on the other side of the room. Susan smiled and rushed off, trying to memorize everything she was seeing.

She could hear Brandon making small talk with Ed as she made her way into the kitchen. The hardwood floor needed refinishing, and the chipped white counter tile was as colorless as the rest of the kitchen. Glancing around, she couldn't find anything notable that might have caught a young child's attention—no funny kitchen roosters or memorable cookie jar, just a bland kitchen with the bare necessities.

Susan realized she really did need to use the bathroom, so she walked through the kitchen to the door leading to the small room.

Sitting on the commode, her shorts at her ankles, Susan glanced around the tiny room. Sarah hadn't mentioned anything about visiting the bathroom at the woman's house, so Susan didn't imagine she'd find anything in this room that might jog Sarah's memory.

Reaching for the toilet paper, Susan glanced down at the trashcan beside the toilet. Frowning, Susan looked into the can. *Is that what I think it is?* she asked herself.

<hr>

"THANK YOU FOR LETTING ME USE YOUR BATHROOM," Susan said brightly as she reentered the room clutching her purse.

"That was quick," Brandon mumbled, eyeing Susan curiously.

Still smiling, Susan snatched Brandon's hand, pulling him to the front door as she chattered away, explaining how she needed to get back to the camp while again thanking Mr. Summers for the use of his bathroom.

"What was that all about?" Brandon asked once they were back in the truck.

"I found this." Susan pulled what appeared to be a wad of toilet paper from her purse. Gingerly she unfolded the paper to reveal what she had tucked inside.

"Is that what I think it is?" Brandon reached out and picked up what appeared to be a lock of his niece's blonde hair.

"It was in the bathroom trashcan."

CHAPTER TWENTY-TWO

A late morning breeze moved through the pine trees, cooling the warm summer day. Overhead, white puffy clouds dotted the blue sky. In the nearby trees, birds chirped and squirrels scurried up branches.

The only vehicles they saw were those parked in cabin driveways or in the street. They passed one jogger who was going in the opposite direction. She gave Brandon and Susan a little wave as she passed.

The heavy scent of pine triggered Susan's childhood memories of Camp Shipley—fond memories— and she hated the way the wad of tissue paper with Sarah's hair made this place feel ugly and unsafe.

"Are you going to call the sheriff's office now?" Susan asked Brandon as they walked to the front door of his cabin.

"First I want to talk to Kit. I think the sheriff's

office should know, but what they'll actually do at this point… probably nothing."

"What do you mean?" Susan looked up at Brandon.

"If you think about it, what crime has been committed? Not saying a crime wasn't committed, especially if the woman tried to abduct Sarah, but what can we really prove?"

"The very least, it'll make them more aware of Harriett Summers' inappropriate behavior."

"Oh, I agree with that. I'm not saying we won't be talking to the sheriff's office, but in the big picture, I'm not sure how much good it'll do, and frankly, it makes staying up here uncomfortable for me, knowing that woman is just around the corner. What in the world did she intend to do with Sarah after she cut off all her hair?"

"Are you saying you might go home early?" Susan asked as they stood by the front door of his cabin.

"I don't know. I've made some commitments here, work I've agreed to do, but under the circumstances… Sarah's safety comes first."

"I guess I understand that." Susan glanced over to the Lewis cabin where her car was still parked. "I suppose I should think about heading back to the camp."

"Do you have to go so soon? When do they expect you back?"

"The girls should return from their ride in an hour or so before dinner."

"So why the rush? It isn't even lunchtime yet. Come inside with me; wait for Kit to return so we can talk to her together."

"Are you sure you want me here when you tell her about the hair?"

"I sort of feel like we're in this together."

"Okay." Susan smiled up at Brandon.

Once inside the cabin, Brandon put the tissue with the lock of hair on the fireplace mantle. When he turned around to face Susan, she was standing by the couch watching him. The memory of their night together flashed in his mind. He recalled how eagerly she had opened to him, how they'd made love not just once or twice but three times that night. He'd been celibate since their time together, mostly because he'd been too busy helping his sister through her difficult time but partly because there was only one woman who held his interest these days—Susan.

Lost in her own private thoughts, Susan watched Brandon set the lock of hair—still in the tissue paper —on the mantle. She wasn't prepared when he turned to her and, without warning, took two sudden steps in her direction and pulled her into his arms.

"Brandon!" she cried out; it was more an expression of surprise than protest. He silenced her with a kiss—demanding and urgent. Startled, Susan stood still, her arms at her sides as she passively accepted the kiss.

"Tell me to stop, and I will," he whispered into her mouth a moment later. In response, she wrapped her arms around his neck, pulling him closer. The kiss she returned was neither passive nor timid.

They fell together onto the couch, Susan on top of Brandon. He slipped his hands up her thighs, past the hem of her shorts until his fingertips caressed the lower portion of her buttock cheeks.

"You have the nicest ass," Brandon growled into her ear after his lips left hers. His kisses fell along her jawline and cheek, with nibbles along the earlobe. Susan squirmed on top of him and didn't issue a protest while his hands explored her lower posterior.

"I kind of like yours, too," Susan chuckled, nipping the tender skin along his neck.

"We need to get you out of these damn shorts," Brandon growled, his hands groping to find her zipper.

"I don't think so," Susan said breathlessly, pushing his hand away from the front of her shorts. "Your sister could walk in on us."

"Damn," Brandon grumbled. His hands abandoned her shorts and slipped into her blouse, pulling it upwards, exposing her bra. Susan arched her back, giving him permission to continue. Gently tugging the bra upwards, Brandon freed Susan's breasts from their silky constraints. Eagerly, he seized one nipple in his mouth as his right hand fondled her other breast. Brandon's free hand moved downward, his fingers wiggling their way into her shorts, teasing the tender skin on her belly.

Fevered and ready to lose herself in the moment's passion, she heard a car door slam. Brandon heard it, too. They jumped up from the couch. Hurriedly, Susan pulled her bra back in place and adjusted her clothing before running her fingers through her hair. Somewhere along the way, her ponytail had come undone. She found her scrunchy on the floor by the couch and was just re-securing her ponytail when Kit and Sarah walked into the cabin.

Brandon's and Susan's flushed and somewhat breathless countenances were not lost on Kit, who eyed the two curiously as she walked into the room. Kit noticed Brandon's guilty expression and the awkward way he stood with his hands shoved into the front pockets of his jeans. *Hiding the evidence?* Kit thought with a chuckle.

"What's funny, Mommy?" Sarah asked.

"Nothing dear," Kit said, trying to suppress another chuckle. "Come, let's go in the kitchen, and I'll make you a snack." Kit ushered Sarah from the room.

"That was embarrassing," Susan said, once again adjusting her clothes.

"Just imagine how embarrassing it would have

been if she had arrived a few minutes later." Brandon grinned.

"Oh, you're awful!" Susan laughed.

Brandon reached out and touched her hand. "Yeah, I am. But it's all your fault."

"My fault?" Susan arched her brow.

"Since the first time we met, I wanted to get to know you better."

"You mean get into my pants." Susan chuckled.

"As I recall, you tried to get in my pants before I tried yours." Brandon took her hand in his and gave it a little squeeze. "And you were quite successful at it."

"You aren't going to let me forget it, are you?"

"Not for a minute." Brandon pulled Susan to him and gave her a quick kiss before releasing her.

"When are we going to talk to Kit about what we found?" Susan asked.

"I'll see if she'll bring Sarah in here for her snack and put on a movie so we can talk in the kitchen without her overhearing us."

"Sounds like a good idea."

"You think you can keep your hands to yourself?" Brandon teased.

"What is that supposed to mean?"

"I know I'm irresistible. But I don't want you embarrassing yourself in front of my sister." Brandon grinned.

"Oh, shut up!" Susan laughed, swatting his butt as he turned toward the kitchen.

"See, I knew you couldn't keep your hands off me!" Brandon said with a laugh.

"Is Susan still here?" Kit asked when Brandon walked into the kitchen a moment later. Sarah sat at the kitchen table waiting for her mother to pour a glass of milk and set two cookies on a plate.

"Yes. We wanted to talk to you but wondered if the munchkin would take her snack in the living room with Cinderella."

"Looks like whatever misunderstanding there was between you and Susan is over," Kit whispered.

"Pretty much."

"So, what's the deal?" Kit glanced at the doorway leading to the living room.

"You're nosey." Brandon chuckled.

"I like her, by the way. So does Sarah," Kit said.

"That's good, because so do I."

"Sarah, let's take this in the living room, and you can watch Cinderella." Kit headed to the doorway carrying a glass of milk and plate of cookies.

"OH MY GOD, SARAH WAS TELLING THE TRUTH." KIT stared at the lock of blonde hair, partially wrapped in the crumbled toilet paper. Brandon had set it on the kitchen table before her. Gently she unfolded the paper to better inspect the hair. Susan and Brandon sat down at the table with Kit. Sarah was in the living room, watching a movie and eating cookies.

"You say you found this in that woman's bathroom?" Kit asked.

"Susan did when she used her bathroom. It looks like Sarah's hair to me. The only two people at that cabin are the Summerses—he's bald, and she has gray hair."

"It looks like Sarah's hair, and it's the right length—about what was taken. Of course, if necessary, it can always be tested to prove it's Sarah's. That officer didn't believe us; this will prove Sarah was telling the truth." Kit looked at her brother.

"We have a little problem with that," Brandon said.

"What do you mean?" Kit frowned.

"Apparently, the officer who was here this morning is Harriet Summers' younger brother," Brandon explained.

"I don't understand." Kit looked from Susan to Brandon.

"The woman who cut Sarah's hair," Susan explained. "She's the older sister of the deputy—the officer who talked to Sarah this morning."

Kit hit the table with her fist. "Then we talk to someone else!"

"I agree, but first we need to figure out who we should go to. I don't want this swept under the carpet," Brandon said. The three sat in silence for a few moments, each considering the situation.

"I have an idea," Susan said at last. "Talk to Carol, see who she thinks you should go to with this. She's been coming up here for years. Carol seems to have a good relationship with the local sheriff's office, knows many of the people who own cabins up here. She even knows who Harriet Summers is. In fact, she called her an odd duck. Not only is Carol Kit's friend, it's in Carol's best interest to get to the bottom of this. She's responsible for the safety of all the girls over at Camp Shipley. What the Summers woman did makes her look like someone who was preparing to abduct Sarah. And remember, I ran into Harriet up at Trail's Chapel where she was—by her very words—looking for a little girl. Yet, she denied knowing anything about Sarah."

"Damn. That thought gives me chills. I think you have a good idea, Susan." Kit stood up from the table. "I'm going to put the hair in something, so we don't lose it. I don't want a breeze to whisk it away before we can prove what Sarah said was true." Brandon and Susan watched as Kit took an empty glass jar from the kitchen cabinet and tucked the hair and toilet paper inside the container.

"I'm going upstairs to call Carol. Can you keep an eye on Sarah?" Kit asked.

"Sure, Kitty." Brandon watched his sister leave the room, taking the glass jar with her.

"She's been through so much these last few months," Brandon said after Kit left the room. Susan reached over and placed her hand over his.

"You're a good brother, Brandon."

"Is that why you let me kiss you?"

"That… and the fact I think you're cute."

Brandon laughed.

arriet Summers awkwardly made her way into the cabin, carrying two bags of groceries. The sweat pants and shirt she wore were just one set of four pairs she owned—all the same color blue. It made it easier to do laundry. The strand of pearls around her neck had once belonged to her mother, and before that, her mother's mother. They were to go to her daughter someday, but Harriet Summers no longer had a daughter.

She ignored Ed, who sat in his wheelchair on the other side of the room, and went straight to the kitchen. After setting the groceries on the small oak table, she returned to the living room.

"Do you have more?" Ed asked.

"Three more sacks."

"You know, it would be easier for you to carry in

the groceries if you let them put it in plastic bags instead of paper sacks," Ed reminded.

"You've told me that before. But I don't like plastic bags."

"I don't know why you make things so difficult, Harriet," Ed said with a sigh.

Harriet went back outside to bring in the rest of her groceries while Ed sat in his wheelchair and watched. After she brought in the last bag, Ed followed her into the kitchen.

"I'll make you lunch as soon as I put these away." Harriet hurriedly unpacked the groceries.

"That's okay. I'm not hungry." Ed sat in his wheelchair and watched his wife.

"Did you eat something while I was gone? I told you I'd be back in time to make you lunch."

"I'm perfectly capable of making my own sandwich."

"Well, did you?" Harriet paused for a moment and looked at Ed.

"Did I what?"

"Did you make yourself a sandwich while I was gone?"

"No. But I could have, if I was hungry."

"You always say that, but then you don't eat." Harriet stopped putting away the groceries and started making Ed a sandwich.

"When were you at Trail's Chapel?" Ed asked.

Harriet looked up from the slices of bread she'd

just placed on the counter. "What are you talking about?"

"When did you go up to Trail's Chapel? A woman stopped by this morning and said you'd been up there yesterday afternoon and wanted to make sure you got home okay."

"Then I suppose I must have gone up there yesterday afternoon," she snapped.

"It was raining yesterday afternoon."

"So? I don't melt in the rain." Harriet slapped slices of ham on the bread.

"I don't like you hiking alone."

"I like to hike. And I can't hike with you anymore." Harriet added cheese and mayonnaise to the sandwich.

"And whose fault is it?" Ed snapped.

"I don't want to talk about that," Harriet said, her voice barely a whisper.

"I'm sorry. But really, Harriet, hiking up there during a storm… It isn't safe."

"You said a woman stopped by?" Harriet looked up from the sandwich as if she'd just processed what he'd said about a visitor.

"Yes, she and a man. I don't remember their names."

"Why was she here?" Harriet cut the sandwich in two and set it on a plate.

"I told you, she said she was worried about you, wanted to make sure you were okay."

Harriet handed Ed the plate.

"And that's all? She just stopped by to check on me?"

"So, you do remember meeting someone?" Ed took a bite of the sandwich.

"Yes. She was in the chapel. But I only talked to her for a minute." Harriet frowned. "I never told her my name. How did she know who I was? Where I lived?"

Ed responded with a shrug and took another bite of his sandwich.

"Did she say anything else? Ask you any questions?"

"No, not really. She asked for you, and when I said you weren't here, she asked if you got home alright. That's about all she said."

"She didn't ask you any other questions?"

"No, like I said, she didn't say much beyond that. I chatted a little with her friend when she went to the bathroom."

"Went to the bathroom?"

"Yes. I couldn't very well tell her she couldn't use our bathroom."

"What did you talk to her friend about?" Harriet asked.

"Nothing beyond the weather. Would you pour me a glass of milk?"

"I still would like to know how she found out where I live." Harriet poured a glass of milk and handed it to Ed before going back to putting her groceries away.

"I don't know. Is there a problem?"

"I just don't like strangers following me back to my cabin, invading my privacy."

As Harriet put the rest of the groceries away, Ed finished his sandwich and drank his glass of milk. Harriet neatly folded the empty paper sacks and put them on top of the refrigerator with the rest of the paper bags she'd accumulated. She then took the empty glass from Ed and washed it in the sink. After drying it, she placed it back in the overhead cabinet. Without saying anything to her husband, she walked to the bathroom off the kitchen.

Once inside the bathroom, she closed the door. Sitting on the toilet seat, Harriet thought about the visitor, wondering how and why the woman had tracked her down. Glancing to the sink, she noticed the scissors she'd left there the night before. Looking down at the trashcan, she thought of why she had used the scissors.

It took her brain a moment to register what she was seeing—or more accurately, what she wasn't seeing. Panicked, she hastily finished and quickly hiked up her pants. Standing up, Harriet picked up the trashcan and started rummaging through it. There was the empty toilet paper roll she'd tossed in the can that morning, several tissues she'd used to blow her nose the night before, and several balls of soiled cotton, but there was no blonde hair.

"Ed!" Harriet shouted as she raced from the bathroom. Ed was no longer in the kitchen, but had wheeled himself back into the living room.

"What are you shouting about?" Ed asked, looking up from a book he was reading.

"Did you take anything out of the bathroom trash can?"

"Are you asking if I dumped the trash? No, of course not. You know I can't get out to the garage where we keep the trash cans."

"No, I'm asking if you took anything out of the trash. It hasn't been dumped."

"Why would I take anything out of the trash?" Ed asked incredulously.

"Because something is missing!" Harriet shrieked. "That woman! Oh my god, that woman was in the trash!"

"You aren't making any sense Harriet. Why in the world would that woman want to go through our trash?"

"If you didn't take it, then she must have!"

"What did you do, drop an earring or something in there?"

"Of course not. If I dropped an earring in the trash, I wouldn't have left it in there."

"Then what are you so upset about? I can't

imagine that young woman was digging around in our bathroom trash, but if she did, so what?"

"Ed, you don't understand. You don't understand anything. You never did!" Harriet shrieked.

"What have you done this time, Harriet?" Ed asked in a chilling tone.

"You let the woman in here. This is your fault, Ed. Why do you always do this?"

"What have you done?" Ed again asked.

"Did that woman give you her name?"

"Yes, but I don't remember. Tell me Harriet, what is this about?"

"Please, Ed, for once, help me."

"Isn't that what I've been doing all these years?"

"Please, Ed, try to remember her name."

Ed thought for a moment. *What had the woman said?*

"I remember, she said something about being a counselor at one of the camps."

"Which one?" Harriet asked.

"I don't remember which camp. There are only two up here. Her name was Sally or Susan... maybe Cindy."

"This friend she was with, what did he look like? Do you remember his name?"

"No. She said it so quick. I don't remember. He was a nice looking young man, blond, about Stan's age. What did she take, Harriet? What has you so upset?"

"I want to go home," Harriet blurted out as she paced the living room floor.

"Home? We've only been here a week. What's wrong Harriet? You need to tell me."

"Why, so you can do what?" Harriet spat.

"I don't know. I have no idea what has you so upset. But if you've done something, you need to tell me."

Harriet stared at Ed. She didn't like the way he was looking at her. She'd seen that look before. Of course, he was in a wheelchair now, so what could he really do, she asked herself. However, it was foolish to push him—she'd learned that once before. Taking a deep breath, Harriet forced a smile and tried to appear calm.

"I'm just being silly," she said at last.

"What was in the trashcan?"

"Nothing really—I mean nothing of value. I just know it was fuller—something is missing."

"Are you seriously telling me you got this upset because we have less trash in our bathroom can?"

"When you put it that way, it does sound silly. But I'm always reading how snoopy reporters are going through people's garbage, trying to find secrets."

"Why would…" Ed didn't finish his sentence.

"Yes, why would anyone want to rummage through our garbage?" Harriet finished the sentence for him. "I'm going upstairs to take a nap. It's been a long day." Without another word, Harriet turned and left the room, making her way up to the bedroom she no longer shared with her husband.

Upstairs, Harriet sat on the side of her bed, picked up the telephone, and dialed her brother's phone number.

Deputy Anderson answered his phone, "Hello?"

"Hi, Jimmy. This is Harriet."

"Hi, Harriet, how are you doing? How is Ed?"

"We're fine. I just wanted to know, did they find that little girl that was missing?"

"Yes. She'd just wandered off from her cabin, found her own way home."

"So she was okay?" Harriet asked.

"Yes, but her mother and uncle called me up there today over some cockamamie story about someone cutting the little girl's hair."

"Cutting her hair? What do you mean?"

"No big deal. A piece of her hair had been cut off; you could barely notice. The kid was probably playing with scissors, and her mother overreacted, insisted someone had cut her hair while she was missing. But the kid came home herself and didn't say anything about anyone trying to take her. Just an overreacting parent."

"I'm glad to hear she's okay. Where is she staying?"

"Not far from you. They're renting the Hunter cabin. The one next to the Lewises'."

"You said her uncle and mother. Doesn't she have a father?"

"No, I guess he was killed a few months back. Some sort of robbery."

"That's so sad… This uncle… what does he look like?"

"Nice looking guy I guess, around thirty, blond. Why?"

"Just curious. Wondered if I've seen him around."

"He was in one of the search parties—teamed up with a counselor over at Camp Shipley to help look for the girl. I guess the gal sprained her ankle a bit, got her stranded up at Trail's Chapel. He went back and got her on horseback. Fortunately that was the extent of any accidents with the search, and according to the doc, she's probably up and running today. Good ending all around."

"You don't happen to know her name?"

"Actually, I do. Susan Thomas. Why?"

"Just curious, Jimmy."

CHAPTER TWENTY-FOUR

"I guess I'll see you over at Carol's office later this afternoon." Susan stood by the side of her car in the Lewises' driveway.

"Thanks for helping us in this." Brandon noticed a lock of Susan's hair had escaped her scrunchy and was about to fall over her right eye.

"Of course, I'll do whatever I can to help. I think Carol had a good idea, meeting at her office. If your sister just showed up at the sheriff's station to talk to Carol's friend, he might not take your concerns seriously. At least Carol can vouch for your sister—and voice her own concerns."

"I agree with you." Brandon leaned toward Susan and brushed the stray lock of hair away from her eye, tucking it behind her ear. He gave her a light kiss on the mouth, and then moved backward. Gazes locked, they were both silent for a few moments before Susan spoke.

"What are we doing, Brandon?" she asked in a quiet voice.

"What do you mean?"

"This… the kisses… the hand holding…"

"I thought we agreed we could start over." Brandon looked slightly confused.

"But what does that mean, start over? There really wasn't an *us* before. I mean, we had that night… but…"

"As I remember, it was a hell of a night." Brandon smiled.

"I agree. But when we first met, you offered to be —what did you call it—a *rebound lover*? Someone between my failed marriage and my next relationship."

"Is that how you see this?" Brandon narrowed his eyes.

"I just want to know how you see this. You wanted honesty, and that's what I am trying to give you—honesty. I don't want to assume one thing and learn later that the reality is something else. I already made that mistake with us once, and I don't want to do it again. I guess what I'm asking, what do you want from us? To be fuck buddies?"

"Did you just say *fuck buddies*?" Brandon about choked on the term. He didn't know if he should laugh, or be pissed. By the blush on Susan's face, it was obvious she'd embarrassed herself.

"Okay… maybe *friend's with benefits.* I don't know; this is a first for me." Susan flushed.

"Now that I think about it, when you approached me at After Sundown, your proposition had nothing to do with a relationship…. more along the fuck buddy lines."

"Oh, shut up!" Susan suddenly wished she'd kept her mouth shut. "Please don't remind me!"

Brandon laughed, then stepped closer and pulled Susan to him. "Sure, I'd love you for a fuck buddy," he whispered in her ear. "Providing I was your *only* buddy."

"I hate that term. I don't even know why I used it."

"Shock value maybe? To get my attention?" Still holding Susan in his arms, he gave her an affectionate squeeze.

"I suppose I want this to be more than that."

"I know we haven't spent much time together. But the more I get to know you, the more I want to spend time with you. I have no idea where this is going, but for me it isn't about some casual relationship—friends with benefits without a commitment."

"What are you saying, Brandon?"

"I'm a little too old to ask you to be my girlfriend," Brandon said with a chuckle. "But I'd like to give the exclusive thing a try. Give us a chance to get to know each other better, see if there is a future for us."

"I remember you saying you weren't looking for a relationship."

"I wasn't. But things have changed. I suppose part of it was losing Kev—being reminded how quickly life can change, the importance of family and friends. And also… I met you. I don't want you to think I suddenly wanted to get into a relationship, that any woman would fit the bill, and that you just happened to be there. More accurately, I suddenly realized I no longer wanted to waste my time on women who only interested me for, for a lack of better word, casual sex."

"I feel the same way. I'd like to see where this thing takes us. But if we're going to be exclusive… I mean…" Susan suddenly grinned mischievously, as if she'd thought of something.

"What?" Brandon asked with a frown.

"I really think you should give me your class ring," she teased.

"Isn't that something they did in our parent's generation?" Brian asked with a chuckle.

"Hey, I'm an old fashioned girl," Susan playfully quipped.

"Okay… if I can find it." Brandon grinned and opened the car door for Susan. After she got in, he closed the door, and she rolled down the window.

"When we get this thing sorted out with Sarah,

we can go on a real date," Brandon said as he leaned against the car door and looked into the open window.

"What would be your idea of a real date?"

"I was thinking fishing—maybe pack a picnic. Do you like to fish?"

"I like to sit by the lake, and I like to eat. But I'll let you do the fishing."

"How about if I bait your hook?"

"You would do that for me?"

"Sure." Brandon grinned.

"It would be very un-feminist of me to let you do that. You wouldn't tease me about it later, would you?"

"Are you kidding me? You'll forever be reminded that I had to bait your hook."

Susan laughed and accepted his quick kiss goodbye.

"Okay, I suppose I can survive the ridicule. But you'll also have to clean any fish I catch."

"Deal. But you'll have to cook them."

"Don't get all chauvinist with me. You'll cook your own damn fish," Susan said with mock indignation.

"Okay, just as long as I know how it is."

Susan flashed Brandon a playful grin before they exchanged their final goodbyes. He stood by the side of the street and watched her drive away.

When Susan arrived back at the camp, she pulled

into the north parking lot and found a vacant spot adjacent to a thicket of pine trees not far from the path leading to the cabins. There were approximately a dozen cars parked in the area and no people in sight.

Standing by the side of her car, she looked out toward the mountain highway and thought about Brandon. In spite of the unsettling information, they'd discovered about Harriet Summers, she couldn't stop smiling. Something deep inside her made a queasy little flip. Susan Thomas felt like a giddy high school girl again.

Taking a deep breath, she started to turn around when she felt something hard nudge the center of her back and heard a female voice say, "Don't move."

Susan froze. *Is that a gun in my back?*

"Now, very slowly, I want you to step backwards and move into the trees with me. Move slowly if you know what's good for you."

Susan was fairly certain she recognized the voice: Harriet Summers. Taking careful, short steps, Susan moved backwards away from the parking lot and into the trees. Frantically, she looked around. The last thing she wanted was for one of the girls to see them and get hurt. *Perhaps it isn't a real gun.*

Walking backwards proved challenging, but she took it one step at a time and tried her best not to stumble into Harriet, who held the gun with what appeared to be a shaky hand.

"Stop. You can turn around now," Harriet ordered when they were concealed within the thicket. Susan turned around and faced the elderly woman who was most definitely holding a real gun.

"Where is it? What did you do with it?" Harriet demanded.

"What are you talking about?" The moment Susan asked the question, she knew the answer—the hair. At the time, she hadn't considered Harriet would notice the hair had been removed from the trashcan, but she now realized her foolish oversight. She herself had told Mr. Summers to let his wife know she'd stopped by. *Stupid. Stupid!*

"You know what I'm talking about. What you took out of the trashcan!"

"What are you talking about?" *I need to play dumb. Make her think her husband removed the hair—anything but me.* "I just stopped by your house to check on you. I was worried that you might not have gotten home okay. I don't know what you think I took, but I would never steal anything."

"I know you used the bathroom. You were the only one who could have taken it."

"I lose things all the time—maybe whatever you think you lost is just misplaced. I didn't take anything out of your house, I promise." *I wonder if I will go to hell for lying under the circumstances. I just hope I don't find the answer to that question in the very near future.*

"Does he have it? Did you give it to him?"

Oh my god, Brandon. I can't let her shoot me and then go after Brandon!

"Whatever you think I took, it can't be worth shooting me over. I mean, if you think I stole something, call the sheriff. Report me. Please. But please not this..."

"You would like that, wouldn't you?"

I guess suggesting calling the sheriff wasn't the best tactic.

"Only because I don't want you to do something you will regret—what we'll both regret. If I knew what you were talking about I would gladly hand it over. Honest. What could I have possibly taken from you that I would be willing to keep and risk getting shot?" *That sounds reasonable to me… if in fact she was missing something of value, like money or jewelry.*

"I don't want to shoot you. I don't want to hurt anyone. I never did."

"Can we talk about it? Let me help you. Tell me what you're looking for. Maybe I saw it in the bathroom when I was there." *Don't they say to get friendly with your kidnaper? Is this what's happening, I'm being kidnapped? Can I continue to maintain this charade, or does she know I'm lying and will it just make her more angry, more apt to shoot me?*

"Give me your purse," Harriet demanded. After Susan handed her the purse, Harriet said, "Now sit down on the ground and don't make any sudden movements." Once again, Susan complied. While keeping hold of the gun, Harriet shakily rummaged through the purse.

"Stand up and empty your pockets," Harriet ordered after tossing the purse on the ground.

Susan stood up and turned her pockets inside out. They were empty.

"You must have given it to him. I knew I should have gone to their cabin before coming here. Start walking." Harriet pointed down the trail with her gun.

"Where are we going?" Susan took one tentative step.

"I need to think. I should have flushed it down the toilet. I never wanted to hurt anyone. But this always happens—someone has to butt in and then someone gets hurt. This is your fault, you know. If you would have simply minded your own business none of this would have happened."

CHAPTER TWENTY-FIVE

They scheduled the meeting at Carol's office to take place an hour after Susan returned to Camp Shipley. Susan had wanted to change her clothes and freshen up before talking with the sergeant, and she planned to meet Brandon, Kit and Sarah at Carol's office at the designated time.

Brandon was a little surprised Susan wasn't waiting for him at Carol's when he arrived but wasn't overly concerned considering her cabin was just a short walk away.

After introductions, Carol suggested having Sarah go with her assistant into the next room so the adults could first talk with Sergeant Grant. He could ask Sarah questions after he had a better feel for the situation.

Instead of waiting for Susan, Kit told the sergeant how she had discovered Sarah's hair had been cut and why she believed it was done during the time the child was missing. Brandon told of Susan's unusual meeting with Harriet Summers up at Trail's Chapel and how they determined the woman's identity. He then told how Sarah had mentioned the pearls, which made both him and Susan wonder if Harriet had in some way been responsible for cutting the child's hair since she'd obviously been looking for a little girl when Susan ran into her at the chapel. Brandon had just explained how Susan had found the hair in the Summerses' bathroom when there was a knock at the office door.

"That must be Susan," Carol said, standing up. Brandon glanced at his watch and wondered what had taken Susan so long.

When Carol opened the door to the office, it wasn't Susan. It was Lexi Beaumont and two of her bunkmates.

"Lexi, we're in a meeting now," Carol explained. "By the way, have you seen Susan? She's supposed to be at this meeting."

Lexi held up a red purse and said, "That's why I'm here. We found this in the trees by the parking lot. It belongs to Susan. Her car's in the parking lot. We've been looking for her—she's not at the cabin, and we can't find her anywhere. We were hoping you knew where she was."

Carol took the purse and ushered Lexi and the

other girls into the office. Both the sergeant and Brandon stood up.

"I don't understand; how can she be missing? You said her car is in the parking lot." Brandon said as Carol looked inside the purse and removed a wallet. She opened it.

"It's Susan's," Carol confirmed. She handed the purse to the sergeant.

"Show me where you found this," Grant instructed Lexi. She nodded and then led him and the rest of the group from the office.

"We were standing here," Lexi explained a few minutes later as they stood at the edge of the north parking lot adjacent to the thicket of pine trees. "We had just got back from the trail ride and sort of expected to find Susan at the cabin. When she wasn't there, we walked out to the parking lot to see if her car was here."

"I noticed the purse," Andrea spoke up. "But I didn't know it was a purse. I just saw something bright red through the trees and was curious."

"Show me where you found it exactly," the sergeant said. "But the rest of you, stay here."

Andrea and the officer moved through the trees until they reached the area where the purse had been found. The ground showed evidence of footprints. Going down on one knee, the officer took a closer look.

"It appears there were two people," the sergeant

said when he and Andrea returned to the group. "The footprints lead off into the forest, away from camp and the cabins. Considering the rain we had yesterday, they must be fresh."

Overwhelmed with a sick sensation—not much different from how he'd felt when he'd learned of Kevin's murder—Brandon panicked. The first thought that popped into his head was that Harriet Summers was responsible for Susan's disappearance, yet why the woman would take her didn't make sense to him. Before he had time to analyze the situation or voice his concerns, a sheriff's vehicle turned into the parking lot and pulled up to where the sergeant was standing. The car came to a stop and the driver rolled down the window. It was Deputy Anderson. The sergeant leaned into the car.

"I thought that was you standing there," Anderson said. He'd noticed his supervisor when driving down the road. "I was getting ready to radio you."

"What's going on?" the sergeant asked.

"I got a call from my brother-in-law, Ed, about thirty minutes ago. Seems some gal, who claims to be a counselor from one of the local camps, stopped by their place looking for Harriet this morning. He let her use their bathroom and now his gun is missing. He keeps it in a drawer in the kitchen."

"Really?" the sergeant glanced over his shoulder at Brandon who was standing out of earshot, talking frantically to Kit and Carol. He looked back at Anderson.

"And what does your sister say? Maybe she moved it."

"Harriet's not home right now; I couldn't ask her."

"Where is she?"

"Ed said she went hiking about an hour ago. But I can't imagine why she'd move the gun. They always keep it in the same place. I bet if we locate that woman and the man who was with her, we'll find the gun."

"I'm pretty sure I know who stopped by your sister's house," the sergeant said, standing up straight. "Jim, I think we need to have a talk."

KIT AND SARAH STAYED WITH CAROL WHILE BRANDON went with the sergeant and Anderson to question Ed Summers. Fortunately, it was dinner hour, making it easier for Carol to gather the girls in one location. She didn't want them wandering around the camp if there was some unbalanced woman with a gun holding one of her counselors hostage. Sarah was excited to eat dinner with all the girls and wasn't aware of the unfolding drama. The sergeant only allowed Brandon to come with him because he didn't want Brandon to take off and search for Harriet and

Susan on his own—assuming, of course, the women were together.

"That's the man who was here today!" Ed said the minute Brandon walked into his cabin with the two officers. "You're quick, Jim. Did you get my gun back? Why isn't he in handcuffs?"

"Just a minute, Ed," the sergeant said. "Did Harriet get back yet?"

"Harriet? No, she went hiking. But, I'd prefer she not know about this. As it is, she was angry at me for letting them in here. Why isn't he in handcuffs?"

"We don't think he or his friend took your gun," Jim said, his voice shaky. "Ed, where is my sister?"

"I told you, she went hiking. And of course, they took my gun. Where is the woman?"

"I think Harriet might have her. We need to figure out where she may have gone. I don't want anyone to get hurt," Anderson said.

"What are you talking about?" Ed said angrily.

"My name is Brandon Carpenter," Brandon spoke up. "My sister and I rented a cabin up here for the summer. Yesterday, my four-year-old niece—my sister's daughter—went missing. While searching for her, Susan, the woman you met this morning, ran into your wife up at Trail's Chapel. Your wife claimed to be looking for her granddaughter."

"We don't have a granddaughter," Ed said.

"Yes, I know. After Sarah was found, my sister noticed someone had cut off a lock of her hair.

According to Sarah, a woman—a woman wearing pearls—found her and promised to take her home. Instead, she took her to a cabin and started to cut off her hair. Sarah was frightened, and when something interrupted the woman and she left the room for a moment, my niece managed to escape. When we came here today, my friend found a lock of Sarah's hair in the trashcan in your bathroom. My friend is missing. We think your wife has taken her."

During Brandon's telling of the events, Ed's complexion lost all color.

"Oh my god, Harriet… what have you done?" Closing his eyes, Ed dejectedly bowed his head.

"What's going on, Ed?" Jim asked, leaning by the wheelchair.

"Harriet never got over losing Terri," Ed said at last. Terri was their young daughter who had drowned during a visit to the beach when the child was in kindergarten. "I can't do this… I can't lie anymore."

"What does this have to do with Terri?" Anderson asked.

"I didn't know how bad it was for Harriet… not until the Collins girl."

"The Collins girl? Are you talking about the little girl that went missing—what fifteen, sixteen years ago?" the sergeant asked.

"I wasn't here—wasn't at the cabin that weekend.

Harriet came up to Shipley that weekend alone. When she came home, she had a little girl with her."

"Are you saying my sister took the Collins girl?"

"She told me the little girl was being abused—that she saw the aunt hit her. She said they didn't deserve to have such a perfect little girl. It took me a minute for it to register—Harriet had kidnapped the child. She seemed to have no idea the severity of the situation. I realized she needed help. I told her she had to take the child back, that we would get her help."

"What happened?" Brandon asked, knowing the child's body had been left at a church.

"She wouldn't listen to me. I started to take the child downstairs. I didn't want them to lock Harriet up—I just wanted to get her help. I decided to leave the little girl at the police department, tell them I found her."

"But you left her body instead at the church," Brandon snapped.

"No. No… Harriet flew at me… she was so angry. She accused me of taking another child away. She blamed me for Terri drowning—said I didn't keep a close enough eye on her. Perhaps she was right. We fell down the stairs. It killed the little girl, and me…"

"It damaged your spinal cord," Anderson finished for him.

"When I woke up, Harriet was beside my bed in the hospital. I asked her where the child was. She told me she'd dropped her off at a church. At the time, I assumed the little girl was alive… that Harriet had dropped her off at the church like I had intended to drop her off at the police station. It was much later that I discovered she had died. She was killed during the fall."

"Oh my god…" Jim stood up and walked to the couch. Sitting down he put his hands over his face and shook his head.

"We have to find them. She's obviously figured out Susan took that hair," Brandon said in a panic.

"I don't believe Harriet meant to hurt your niece. I think she was cutting her hair to change her appearance. She just wanted a little girl to love. I don't believe she'll hurt your friend," Ed insisted.

"Your wife has a gun, and I believe she has Susan," Brandon said angrily.

CHAPTER TWENTY-SIX

The woman was ranting. She had been ranting for the past forty or more minutes, struggling to decide what she should do. Susan stopped trying to talk to her because, each time she said something, Harriet would point the gun at her face and say, "Shut up! I need to think!"

They were walking away from the camp and Susan's ankle started to throb. It had felt fine when she got up that morning, but she had obviously over-taxed the recently injured ankle.

Harriet stopped walking for a moment and ordered Susan to stop. A few yards up the trail was a cutoff that would take them to the highway, yet she didn't think Harriet was going to turn in that direction. If they continued on this trail, they would be deep in the forest by nightfall. Susan needed to do something—*quick.*

"Can we walk a little slower please?" Susan asked. "I hurt my ankle yesterday. That's why I was at Trail's Chapel when you saw me. I was waiting for my friends."

Harriet looked down at Susan's feet, remembering the younger woman had mentioned the ankle when they'd met at the chapel.

"Which one is it?" Harriet asked, leaning down to have a closer look as she absently clutched the gun in her right hand.

Instead of answering Harriet's question, Susan lunged toward the older woman, grabbing for the gun and using the weight of her body to force Harriet to the ground.

THE SERGEANT STOOD BY HIS CAR IN THE SUMMERSES' driveway talking on the radio, summoning reinforcements for a search party. He couldn't use civilians or elicit help from the camps, as he believed Harriet was armed and possibly dangerous. He had already ordered Anderson to return to the station—he was off the case; they couldn't risk a conflict of interest.

He was just getting off the radio when he heard it —a gun shot. The sound reverberated through the mountains.

"That sounded like a gun," Brandon said in a panic. Without a second thought, he got into the passenger's seat of the sheriff's car as Grant got into the driver's seat. They raced out of the driveway and headed in the direction where they believed the sound might have come from.

Brandon spotted them first—two women stumbling down the highway, each covered in mud. He didn't see any gun, and it appeared Susan, who had a noticeable limp, was helping the older woman walk. They looked like a couple of drunks. The moment the sergeant noticed the pair, he turned on the siren and raced in their direction, bringing the vehicle to an abrupt stop less than a yard away from the women.

The sergeant had already drawn his gun when two sheriff's deputies' cars arrived on the scene and parked nearby.

"It's in my back pocket," Susan explained, putting her hip out a bit, so the sergeant could retrieve the gun. Grant reached over and snatched the firearm from Susan's pocket. Brandon took hold of Susan as the sergeant took Harriet into his custody and placed her in the back seat of one of the other sheriff's cars.

Susan slumped against Brandon, closing her eyes as he held her in his arms.

"Are you okay?" he whispered, holding her tight.

"I was scared as hell, and my ankle hurts again. But, yeah, I think I am okay."

When Grant returned to her, she reached into her pocket, pulled out several bullets, and handed them to him.

"What happened?" Grant asked.

"Susan, this is Sergeant Grant," Brandon introduced.

"Harriet figured out I took Sarah's hair from her house. She surprised me by the parking lot when I returned from Brandon's. She had a gun, searched my purse and pockets. When I didn't have it, she started freaking out, realizing I'd probably left it with Brandon. She wasn't sure what she wanted to do, so she made me go with her while she figured it out.

"She started ranting. Didn't make any sense. We were near the cutout to the highway, and I knew I had to do something. I couldn't go with her into the forest. I asked her if we could slow down a little because of my ankle. When she leaned over to look at it I... I grabbed for the gun. In the struggle, it went off."

"You could have been shot," Brandon said as his face went ashen.

"I didn't even think about it; I just reacted. It all happened so fast. The gun went off, and then she freaked out. After I got the gun, I took the bullets out... and, well...here we are."

"She didn't try to get it back from you?" Grant asked.

"No. At that point, it wasn't difficult to get her to come with me. I think with the gun going off, some-thing inside her seemed to snap.

SWAYING GENTLY, THE ALUMINUM FISHING BOAT KEPT ITS place in the bay, secured by the anchor Brandon had tossed into the water just minutes earlier. Cushions, which doubled as life preservers, made the bench seats bearable for the two anglers. As promised, Brandon baited Susan's hook. However, she was more curious about the contents of the wicker picnic box than what was happening to her pole. It sat forgotten, leaning against the inside wall of the small boat, its line in the water.

"You know, some fish is going to grab your bait and steal your pole," Brandon teased as he reeled in his line before casting again.

"Did you see what your sister put in here?" Susan asked, clearly not concerned with her fishing pole as she rummaged through the picnic basket.

"I know she made chicken."

"Fried chicken… homemade! Oh, it looks so good. Potato salad… and what is this, chocolate cake?"

"Kit likes to cook," Brandon said with a shrug.

"I love your sister. That lady knows how to put together a picnic." Susan closed the basket and set it on the floor of the boat. She looked over at Brandon. "It really was sweet of her to do this for us."

"I told her we were going on our first real date,

and after I mentioned where I intended to take you, she offered to put the basket together."

"I was expecting peanut butter sandwiches." Susan got up from her bench seat and moved to where Brandon was sitting, taking her fishing pole and cushion with her. Before sitting next to him, she set the cushion on the bench.

"This is nice, isn't it?" Brandon said a moment later. The two sat side by side, fishing poles in hand.

"I sort of thought you were going to stand me up on our first date," Susan said.

"Why did you think that?"

"When you had to go to town last night, I wasn't sure you'd make it back in time."

"I told you it would be a quick trip—there and back. I had to pick up some tools I forgot, plus a couple other things."

"I'm just glad you made it back in time for our date."

"How does your ankle feel?"

"It's a little sore but much better."

They fished in silence for about ten minutes, each considering the events of the last few weeks.

"What do you think is going to happen to Harriet and her husband?" Susan asked.

"I don't know. That woman has some real problems. At the very least, she'll be institutionalized. Not sure what they'll do with her husband. Poor bastard.

All those years in a wheelchair, and he was just trying to do the right thing."

"I'm just glad that's behind us. I will be perfectly content to spend the rest of the summer drama free."

"You and me both," Brandon agreed, and then added, "But there is one thing."

Brandon set his fishing pole down and stood up. The boat rocked slightly. Susan watched as Brandon dug his right hand into the front pocket of his jeans. She eyed him curiously.

"What are you doing?"

"Here it is," Brandon said with a grin, pulling his hand from his pocket. She couldn't tell what he was holding. He sat back down and looked at her.

"I want to ask you something," Brandon said, still smiling.

"What?"

"I was wondering…" He held out his hand before opening it. "Will you be my girlfriend?" Susan looked down to see what he was offering her. He held a somewhat worn and tarnished gold class ring with a garish red stone.

Susan snatched up the ring and began to laugh as she tried it on. It was much too large for her ring finger so she tried it on her middle finger and then on her thumb.

"Where did you get this?" Susan asked, moving the ring from one finger to the next.

"I picked it up at my house when I stopped to get the tools."

"You are so funny," Susan giggled.

"Well, what do you say?" Brandon asked, his voice now serious. Placing his arm around Susan, he pulled her closer. She leaned on his shoulder as she slipped the ring on her middle finger and closed her hand so the ring wouldn't fall off.

"I'm crazy about you, Susan," Brandon whispered into her ear.

She turned to face him as he lifted his hands and gently cupped her face. They leaned toward each other, and their lips met. Susan closed her eyes, savoring the soft kiss, her lips parting as his tongue teased hers.

"Is it too soon for me to say… I love you?" Susan asked in a shaky whisper when the kiss ended.

"Not soon enough," Brandon murmured before kissing her again.

UNLOCKED ♥ HEARTS

**You met them in *Sundered Hearts*,
now read their stories:
Kit Landon in *After Sundown***

Women don't come to After Sundown for the beer—
they come to get laid. When wealthy Cole Taylor
walks into the bar that night, it's for a drink. He gave
up one-night stands in his wild youth, but that
changes when he sees her. She is too tempting to pass
up, and by the looks from the other men at the bar, he
needs to move quick to claim the prize.

Kit Landon—a struggling young widow, raising
her daughter alone—has her own reasons for being at

After Sundown. And it has nothing to do with illicit sex. But things can escalate a little too fast after nervously downing several beers on an empty stomach.

The conservative young widow finds herself in an extremely compromising situation and barely manages to escape, leaving behind a furious Cole Taylor.

Kit never wants to see the man again, but she is in for a big surprise.

Ella Lewis in
While Snowbound

Snowbound with the famous rocker might be her best friend's fantasy, but it isn't Ella's. Nor is she impressed with the fact Brady Gates was voted sexiest man of the year—twice. Ella was looking forward to the isolation of her mountain cabin and the peace and quiet she needs to finish writing her book. Rescuing the careless celebrity in the midst of a blizzard and taking him to the safety of her remote cabin was not how she intended to spend her time on the mountain.

Weary of lovestruck fans climbing into his bed uninvited and the ever-present paparazzi, Brady

Gates had planned to take an incognito break from his hectic life and spend several weeks alone at a remote mountain cabin.

Finding himself stranded in a blizzard doesn't bother him half as much as the fact the one woman he wants is the one woman who is the least interested in him.

Lexi Beaumont in
Sugar Rush

When Lexi Beaumont refuses to marry the man of her grandfather's choosing, she is banished from her home and stripped of all her belongings. Being abandoned by the manipulative and selfish man who raised her is not especially traumatic—she's been looking for a way to leave her grandfather's home, and was grateful for the college education he provided.

What she wasn't prepared for was her grandfather's attempt to sabotage her efforts at finding a job, nor did she realize he'd hired a man to spy on her.

Needing to regroup, Lexi and her best friend flee

to Lake Havasu City, Arizona, believing it would be one place her grandfather would not look.

She discovers a sweet path to financial security with the help of the supportive and handsome neighbor, who is also new to Havasu. What she doesn't know is that he's been hired by her grandfather.

HAUNTING DANIELLE

The Ghost of Marlow House

The Ghost Who Loved Diamonds

The Ghost Who Wasn't

The Ghost Who Wanted Revenge

The Ghost of Halloween Past

The Ghost Who Came for Christmas

The Ghost of Valentine Past

The Ghost from the Sea

The Ghost and the Mystery Writer

The Ghost and the Muse

The Ghost Who Stayed Home

The Ghost and the Leprechaun

The Ghost Who Lied

The Ghost and the Bride

The Ghost and Little Marie

The Ghost and the Doppelganger

The Ghost of Second Chances

The Ghost Who Dream Hopped

THE GHOST OF CHRISTMAS SECRETS

THE GHOST WHO WAS SAY I DO

THE GHOST AND THE BABY

THE GHOST AND THE HALLOWEEN HAUNT

www.ingramcontent.com/pod-product-compliance
Lightning Source LLC
Chambersburg PA
CBHW050339190726

48284CB00007BB/2074